JASPER

The Dog Who Knew Too Much

JASPER

The Dog Who Knew Too Much

MARIE WOODWARD

XULON PRESS

Xulon Press
2301 Lucien Way #415
Maitland, FL 32751
407.339.4217
www.xulonpress.com

Unless otherwise indicated, Scripture quotations taken from the King James Version (KJV) – *public domain.*

The characters, names, places, and events in this story are purely fictional and do not represent anyone real or living.

Printed in the United States of America.

Paperback ISBN-13: 978-1-6322-1225-2
eBook ISBN-13: 978-1-6322-1226-9

TABLE OF CONTENTS

1. Dreams of a Spiritual Nature. 1

2. A Different Attitude. 3

3. Bad News 8

4. Nothing Can Stop Me 14

5. Getting it Straight 17

6. Walking Out. 21

7. Take Time to Argue 26

8. Another Strange Dream. 30

9. No Need For Groceries Today. 34

10. Watching for the Demon Lady 36

11. Saving a Beautiful Spirit 40

12. Jasper Has Other Plans 51

13. Jasper Plays Both Sides. 53

14. Jasper Only Escapes on Sundays. 59

15. The Dreamer Gets Dreamed 64

16. Jasper Executes Plan B 67

17. The Demon Lady and Mr. Hillbilly go to Church 72

18. Jasper Gets Busted 81

19. A Brand-New Day 87

20. The Chance 89

21. Time to Go 94

22. That's the Way it is 96

23. Leaving Breezewood 100

24. The Letter With No Stamp 102

25. The Final Dream 105

26. No Time for Speed Limits .109

27. The Return of Faith 112

28. Ellie Needs a Miracle 114

29. The Town Comes Together 119

30. A Lesson Learned 123

31. The Funeral-Wedding 126

About the Author 129

Books for Pet Loss and Proof of the Afterlife for
    Animals: 131

References: 135

"Who can find a virtuous woman?
For her price is far above rubies."

(Proverbs 31:10)

Chapter One

DREAMS OF A SPIRITUAL NATURE

Ellie found herself in the vacant house behind hers. Belle was with her and the lights were on. That's odd she thought, *no one lives here but the living room light was on and the room was fully furnished, leaning towards a man's taste.* Belle was whining and looking around as though she could see something that Ellie couldn't.

There was a sliding glass door in the kitchen that looked out into the backyard. Belle walked over to the glass door and began to whine with her ears and tail standing straight up. The porch light was on and it cast a dull, amber color across the backyard. Ellie cautiously walked over to where Belle stood and stopped beside her. "What is it girl?"

Ellie peered out the glass door and she could see the tall, weathered fence and the unkempt bushes that grew in front of the fence. The overgrown bushes looked eerie in the yellowish light and the slight breeze moved the shadows of the trees in a ghostlike manner. Suddenly, she was gripped with fear, *What was she doing here? She should be home, but she was in the empty house…or was it?*

Ellie woke up and realized she had been dreaming about Belle again. She looked at the clock and it was two o'clock in the morning. She rolled over and went back to sleep.

Chapter Two

A DIFFERENT ATTITUDE

The next morning Ellie was sitting at her desk sipping on a cup of coffee staring out the window, pondering the strange dreams she had been having of her dog Belle, who had died almost two months ago. Maybe she should go to the doctor and get something to help her sleep, and yet she was intrigued with the strange dreams. *Did they mean something?* It was always the same dream but each time it progressed like someone reading a book to her; one chapter at a time.

It was late March and spring was finally here after a brutal and lonely winter. As she stared at the huge maple tree in her backyard she could see small, green buds sprouting from the bare branches. Several birds were running around in the yard flitting from place to place. Ellie set her cup down and put both elbows on top of the desk. Cupping her chin in both hands, she took a deep breath and exhaled. The past winter had been very depressing, and it had seemed as though it would never end.

Ellie Simpson was thirty years old and she was a beautiful woman. She was tall and slender, and she stood at five-feet eight-inches. Her long, blonde, curly hair spilled downward onto her slim shoulders cascading around her flawless, tan face. Her nose was long and slim and her big, round, green eyes were adorned with long lashes. When she smiled, her teeth gleamed behind her full lips making her even more beautiful. She was extremely intelligent, and she had a great sense of humor.

She had been divorced from her husband for over two years. Her ex-husband James had met another woman and they had run off to New York together, leaving Ellie with a broken heart. It turned out that James, his lawyer, and Ellie's lawyer were friends, which she didn't find out until after everything was said and done. She had lost almost everything to her husband and at one point she was so angry and frustrated, that she told James he could have whatever he wanted except Belle. Her sense of humor had slowly diminished after all that had transpired in the last few years and she had become cynical and untrusting of men.

After the divorce, they sold their house and Ellie bought the house that she was living in now. It was a modest two bedroom house that was just outside of town and the closest house to hers was the vacant one behind her, which was a fair distance away from her house. The two backyards butted up against each other and were separated by a tall, wooden fence. The houses on each side of her were almost a quarter mile away and Ellie loved the privacy that the location gave her, and it was close to town.

Sometime later after her divorce, she began to date again and that didn't work out well either. She had caught her new boyfriend cheating and she decided that she was through with all men and had concluded that all men were worthless. She swore she would never be with another man again as long as she lived.

A few months after breaking up with her boyfriend she lost her beloved dog Belle to cancer. Belle was a black and white Siberian Husky and she had the most beautiful ocean-blue eyes that shined like crystals. Ellie said that she could see the intelligence in her eyes and Belle had been her best friend, and now she was gone.

Belle had advanced bone cancer and Ellie had to put her to sleep. It had been an agonizing and heartbreaking decision, but she didn't want to be selfish and allow Belle to suffer any longer. Ellie knew that love could be selfish, and she didn't want her need for Belle's love, to dominate the horrific pain that Belle must have been in. She knew she had made the right decision but still, she felt guilty. Belle was nine years old when she passed and now Ellie was lonely. She wanted to adopt another dog to keep her company, but she wasn't sure if the time was right because she was still mourning Belle.

She had seen a stray dog around town and had tried to catch it several times, but the dog was too elusive.

Ellie believed in God, but sometimes wondered if he was real. She had stopped attending church a few years ago and felt ashamed for not attending on a regular basis. When she was a young girl she had faith that could move mountains but living in the real world had stripped her of that, and she wasn't sure anymore if there really was a God. She often wondered that if there really was a God, would he be mad at her for putting Belle down. This ate at her mind often, but she believed that allowing Belle to suffer was wrong. She believed that if Belle could've talked, she would have told Ellie to go ahead and send her on to the afterlife, or wherever dogs go when they pass. Ellie liked to believe that they went to Heaven.

Her father had been in the military and when he left the service they had moved to the small town of Breezewood where he went to work at a local steel plant. Two years later he died of cancer and at the time, Ellie was only ten years old, leaving Ellie and her mother alone to fend for themselves. The cancer took him quickly and it took less than six months from the time he was diagnosed, until he passed. It was a shock to Ellie, and that was the day she lost her faith.

Ellie faithfully visited her mother Joan every Saturday and when she looked up at the clock on the mantel, she saw it was already past one o'clock and she had to be at her mother's house by two. She had spent the morning reflecting on her crazy dream and if she were late, her mother would begin to worry, and she would call Ellie to see if she were alright.

As she was starting to rise from the desk she saw something out of the corner of her eye. She quickly looked through the window into the backyard and she saw Belle standing on the right side of the small greenhouse facing the tall privacy fence, as though she were looking towards the vacant house behind hers. Belle then turned her head and looked at Ellie. Ellie blinked her eyes and looked again, but Belle was gone. She thought, *it must have been her imagination due to grief.* She was well aware that grief could do funny things to your mind, like playing tricks with your eyes, and causing vivid dreams. Ellie told herself, *I won't succumb to crazy thoughts.*

Chapter Three

BAD NEWS

Johnathan Slade didn't like to be around crowds these days, or people in general for that matter, and he had become what many called a loner.

His wife and two daughters had been killed over two years ago in a head-on collision while Johnathan was serving in Iraq, and at the time he thought he was going to lose his mind. When he was given the news, he just sat down in the hot sand in shock and pulled out their pictures and stared at them.

He remained in that position until later that night when he got up and began walking across the desert and nonchalantly walked into an enemy camp where he knew they were holding some of his comrades prisoner. He took out all four combatants, thereby saving his friends lives. One of the combatants got a shot off and the bullet creased the left side of his head leaving a scar almost two inches long just above his ear, where hair now refused to grow. He spent three days in the hospital and was released back to duty, being awarded a Purple Heart and a Silver Cross.

While in Iraq, Johnathan had been a demolitions expert and his partner and best friend was a dog named Sneaky Pete, and his job was to sniff out potential explosives, and Johnathan would disarm and dispose of them. Johnathan called him Petey, and he knew that their spirits had bonded when they first met and had only grown stronger due to all they had gone through as soldiers.

Sneaky Pete was part German Shepherd and part Wolf. He was a massive dog and his fur was gray and black, and his beautiful amber-colored eyes had a strange shine to them, so much so that they looked like glass. He was fiercely loyal and protective of Johnathan and would not let anyone hurt him.

When Johnathan first arrived in Iraq he was ordered to go to the Service Kennel and pick out a dog. Upon entering the kennel, the first dog he noticed was Sneaky Pete. The dog was huge and the instant he and Petey locked eyes they bonded, and he knew this was the dog for him. Johnathan pointed at Petey. "I'll take that one."

The man in charge of the kennel looked at him and laughed saying, "soldier, you don't want that dog he's plumb crazy, nobody wants that one. He's been here for a long time and he likes to eat people. The Captain is thinking about getting rid of him."

"I'll take him."

"What?" the man said staring at Johnathan as if he were crazy.

"I said, I'll take the big one," Jonathan repeated pointing at Sneaky Pete.

"Ok buddy, it's your funeral." He laughed and shook his head. "You can go in there and get him, I'm not going near him. I got to see this. That dog has bitten everyone who has ever tried to put a collar on him." He handed Johnathan a harness and leash, and smiling he said, "good luck!"

Johnathan opened the gate and closed it behind him. He stood there extending his hand towards Petey coaxing him. "Come on boy. Come on, we got work to do." He asked the man what the dog's name was, and the man told him his name was Sneaky Pete. "Come on Petey, come on." Petey slowly walked over to Johnathan and sniffed his hand and then Johnathan began to pet and reassure him. After a brief period, he put the harness on Petey while still talking to him and when he was finished, he opened the gate and thanked the man and he and Petey walked out the door. The man watched them go out the door with a shocked look on his face, and then shook his head and muttered to himself, "well, I'll be." From that day on they were inseparable.

One day while Johnathan and Sneaky Pete were on patrol searching for underground explosives, an Iraqi soldier had suddenly appeared from out of one of the war-ravaged buildings taking Johnathan by surprise. Johnathan saw the man raise his arm back in an attempt to throw a home-made explosive device at Johnathan, but Petey was faster. Sneaky Pete saw the man and charged him, causing the combatant's aim and projected energy to waver. This caused the explosive to fall short of its intended aim and Sneaky Pete took most of the blast and was killed instantly. Johnathan was forcefully blown off his feet and landed backwards on a large pile of rubble breaking his back and taking several pieces of shrapnel to his face. This latest injury had put him in the base hospital where he lay in a coma for two days.

When Johnathan woke up he learned that his back was broken, he was paralyzed from his waist down, and Petey had been killed in the explosion while saving his life. Several weeks later they shipped him to the VA Hospital in Breezewood. His family was gone and now Petey was gone too. He had no other family and he was alone in a strange place, and there wasn't a day that went by that he didn't wonder why all those that he had loved were taken from him, and yet he was still alive.

Johnathan was lying in bed trying to grasp all that had happened when he saw a tall man in a white lab coat enter the room. Johnathan looked at him and guessed him to be about sixty years old. The man was tall and clean shaven, and his hair was grey and thinning on top. He wore a pair of silver, round-rimmed glasses and Johnathan assumed he was a doctor. The man walked over to the bed where Johnathan was and smiled down at Johnathan.

"Hello John, I'm Doctor William Bennett and I'll be taking care of you. You can call me Bill, and if there's anything I can do for you, just let me know." He put his head down and then looked back at Johnathan. "I'm truly sorry about your family and your dog."

"You know about them? My family and Petey?"

"John, I've read all your records and I know you were at the end of your first tour when your family was killed in a head-on collision by a man who had been drinking and had crossed into their lane. I also know that's why you signed up for a second tour, and why you marched into an enemy camp saving your fellow soldiers. You were shot, and that's how you got that scar on the side of your head. The bullet only creased you, but another quarter inch and you would have been dead. I don't know if you were stupid, brave, or blessed; or maybe all three."

"After my family was killed, I guess I just didn't care if I lived or died anymore."

"Are you a Godly man John?"

"Yes, but sometimes I wonder."

"Have you lost your faith?" the doctor asked.

"My family was killed, my dog is dead, and now I can't walk but I still retain my faith. It's been hard and I've had times where I doubted God, but yes I still have my faith."

"That's what I wanted to hear. I'll be taking care of you, so don't give up on me John."

After the doctor left the room, Johnathan stared out the window and wished he had died with Petey and his family. His eyes began to well up and tears began to slowly roll down his cheeks. He turned his face to the wall. *Why Lord? Why did you take away all those that I loved? Why have you allowed me to live?*

Chapter Four

NOTHING CAN STOP ME

Later that afternoon as Johnathan lay in bed, he heard a gentle rap on the door to his room and he said, " come in, it's open." A man in a Captain's uniform peered around the side of the door.

"May I come in John?"

"Yes sir, please come in."

The Captain took off his hat and walked over to the bed. "Mind if I sit?"

"Help yourself sir."

"My name is Captain Wenzel, but please call me Doug. You're a civilian now and there's no need for formalities. I have your discharge, honorable of course, along with a medal that you've been awarded. I know this medal won't bring back your family or Petey, but you've given all for your country and you deserve it. You've been awarded another Purple Heart and I'm honored to be the one to present it to you. You've been quite the soldier and your country owes you a debt of gratitude that can never be repaid. So, I thank you on behalf of the country."

"Thank you sir."

"Oh, one more thing," he said smiling. "Petey has been awarded a Sliver Cross too, which I hope you will accept for him."

Johnathan's face lit up and he looked at the officer. "Thank you sir, he certainly deserved it. He saved my life and he would be happy knowing he received a medal."

"Yes, he died saving your life and that is a true friend and soldier."

"This makes my day sir." Johnathan was so proud of Petey at that moment that he actually smiled.

"I figured it would." Captain Wenzel hesitated and then said, "they say you may never walk again. I'm sorry to hear that."

Johnathan looked over at the officer and said, "I'm going to walk again, and nobody can stop me. My determination and faith will get me up out of this bed, you wait and see!"

"You know John, somehow I really believe that and if you need anything, just ask. Goodbye John. I'll say a prayer for you."

"Thank you sir."

The Captain got up and nodded his head and putting his cap on, he saluted Johnathan and then turned and walked out the door.

Soon after the Captain left, the doctor came back in and sat down in the chair beside Johnathan's bed and leaning forward, he gave Johnathan a serious look and said, "John, we can try an operation if you want. It's a tricky operation but there's is a fifty-fifty chance you could walk again but it's your decision, and I can't make any promises that the operation will be successful, but we can try."

"Let's do it. Anything beats laying here like this. I guess the worse that can happen is that I'll be in the same shape I'm in now."

"That's what I thought you'd say, so I scheduled you for an operation early next week. I have a great doctor coming in from another VA Hospital to assist me, and he's one of our best."

"Sure Doc, let's do it."

"Great, I've set up the operation for Tuesday of next week."

Johnathan thought with grim determination, *I'm going to walk again if it's the last thing I do.*

Chapter Five

GETTING IT STRAIGHT

Ellie arrived at her mother's house with five minutes to spare. Her mother greeted her with a kiss and asked her if she was hungry. Joan was Ellie's mother and she was fifty-five years old. She was a beautiful woman and held her age well. Ellie had her blonde, curly hair and beautiful face, but she had her father's tall, slim build.

"I just made some potato soup, are you hungry? "Joan said as they walked back to the kitchen.

"Sure, I could eat some soup."

"How have you been honey?"

"I'm doing ok, trying to stay busy."

"Have you been dating?"

"Mom let's not go through this again," Ellie said exasperated as she set down at the table.

"Well, I'd like some grandchildren if you don't mind, you and I aren't getting any younger you know," her mother said, as she dipped some soup into a white porcelain bowl and then set the bowl down in front of Ellie warning, "be careful it's hot!" The steam from the bowl slowly drifted upward as Ellie stirred it with her spoon.

"Mom, we've been through this before, can we just drop the subject? I don't trust men, and I don't need one," Ellie said with conviction, and then she blew on her soup causing the steam to quickly scatter away from the bowl, and then as Ellie watched, the steam quickly returned back to its slow drift upward.

Her mother stopped and turned to look at Ellie from the stove, putting one hand on her hip and tilting her head she said, "you know, everybody gets jilted before they meet the right one, and you are no exception. You act like you're the only person who's ever been hurt, you need to quit feeling sorry for yourself and get on with your life. I was jilted before I met your father and I had an attitude for a while just like you, but I knew that if I held onto that attitude I would miss the one man that was meant for me. I'm glad I changed my way of thinking or I wouldn't have met your father, and he was a wonderful man. Those men weren't meant for you honey, you need to get back to church and get back with God."

"Where was God when Dad died, or during my divorce? All I saw was a lawyer trying to hit on me."

"Ellie! Don't you talk like that. You know better than to mock God, I raised you better than that. You were special to God when you were a little child."

"Oh, how's that?" Ellie said cynically.

"When you were just a small child and you were just starting to put words together, sometimes you would point to thin air and say "angel". You had no concept of that word, nor had you ever heard the word angel. So, I know God has always had his hand on you."

"I'm sorry Mom, I just want to be on my own. I don't want or need a man right now." Ellie furrowed her brow and said, "I was thinking about adopting another dog and I've seen a stray around town, but I can't seem to catch him."

Her mother rolled her eyes. "A dog is good, but a man is better. A dog can't take care of you or give you children. I want some grandchildren, now quit being selfish and feeling sorry for yourself. You'll get over what's his name. I never did like him anyway. I knew he was no good and I tried to tell you, but you wouldn't listen."

"I was young and naive then, but not anymore. Can we please drop this subject?" Ellie said groaning, and added, "please!"

After they finished eating, they went into the living room and watched TV while they talked. Ellie told her mother that she was having strange dreams of Belle.

"Oh, you have the gift. Your father had it, and you've had the gift since you were a child and those dreams mean something, but it's up to you to figure them out."

"Gift? What gift?" Ellie asked.

"The gift of dreams and knowing things…you know, a spiritual thing or discernment, or whatever you choose to call it. Whatever it is, it comes from God."

Ellie always knew something was different about her since she was a young girl. She knew things that other kids didn't know, and she couldn't understand why the other children didn't know these things too. For her, it was common sense but as she got older she realized she *did* have a gift.

Ellie told her mother that she had to go.

"Ellie could you run by Ed's hardware store and pick me up some mousetraps? These mice are about to eat me out of house and home."

"Sure Mom, I won't be long."

Chapter Six

WALKING OUT

J onathan woke up after the operation and he was in pain
and groggy from the anesthesia. As he lay in his bed half-
awake, he looked out the window to a gray and dreary day,
and he realized it was raining. The pitter-pattering of the
rain caused him to go back to sleep, and he began to dream.
He was with his family in a park that he didn't recognize. It
appeared to be a small park with a river, and he could see a
dam that was about thirty yards down-river. His girls were
playing with Sneaky Pete and he and his wife were talking as
they watched them play. His wife was talking but he couldn't
hear what she was saying, when all at once there was a loud
explosion and the brightness from the blast blinded him.
When he regained his vision, he was desperately looking for
his family and Petey, but he couldn't find them, and he began
to scream their names. He woke up and there was a nurse
beside him, coaxing him to wake up.

Later that day the doctor came in and informed Johnathan that the surgery was successful. Johnathan spent four months in the hospital following his surgery taking therapy and convalescing.

Johnathan was extremely fit before his accident but had lost some weight, which was mostly muscle deterioration from being bedridden. While in Iraq he had exercised and lifted weights daily because staying fit could mean the difference between life or death.

Johnathan was six-feet tall and he had been all muscle before he was confined to the bed. He was thirty-one years old and had dark hair, which had grown long from laying in the bed, and he had a full black beard. His eyes were green, and he had a gentle and contagious smile. His tan, rugged face had two small scars from the shrapnel he had taken in the explosion. One started at the left corner of his mouth and ran about a half an inch towards his chin. The other scar was smaller and started at the top of his right eyebrow and stopped at the top of his eyelid. And like the scar on his head, his eyebrow had a small niche where hair wouldn't grow. On the left side of his head was the small, thin, bare scar where the bullet had whizzed by and burned his head.

One day in late March, the doctor came in to check on him and give him the good news. "You've made remarkable progress John and you've healed nicely."

"I feel great Doc, when can I leave here?"

"Well…how about tomorrow?" he said with a grin.

"Great!" John said enthusiastically, "I'm ready to get out of here. Not that I'm not grateful to you and the staff but I want to go to work, I can't see me sitting around all day. Can I work? I mean, am I able to work?"

"Yes John, but nothing strenuous for a while. Where do you plan to go and where will you stay? I know you have no family. Aren't you're originally from Virginia?"

"Yes, but I don't have any family there now, and I guess I wasn't thinking that far ahead."

"Well, I believe I can help you with that. This is a small community and I think you would like it here if you gave it a chance. I called a friend of mine and explained your situation and he informed me that he had a vacant house for rent, and it's fully furnished if you care to go look at it. May need a little yard work because the house has been vacant for some time, and he said you could move in as soon as you wish. My friend said that since you were a veteran and a war hero, he would give you the first month's rent free.

I also called the Canine Training Center which is about twenty minutes from here and told them I had an expert dog trainer. I told them about your experience, and they said you could start whenever you wished. They said you could start out part-time and go to full-time whenever you are ready, I do have some connections in this town."

"Wow Doc, I don't know what to say," Johnathan said in disbelief.

"Well, I figured anyone who could come back from what you've been through deserves a little help. Oh, and thank the Captain too, he helped," the Doctor said smiling.

"I don't know what to say. Thank you Doctor," Johnathan said humbly.

The Doctor looked seriously at Johnathan. "By the way John, I'm the Pastor at the church here in town and I'll expect to see you there after you've settled into your new place."

John smiled. "Blackmail, eh?"

The doctor smiled back at Johnathan. "Perhaps."

"You're a Pastor too?"

"Yes, in a small town like Breezewood we tend to have a shortage of Doctors and Pastors," he replied with a smile. "I'll see you in church then?"

"Yes sir, I'll be attending as soon as I am settled."

"Oh, by the way, I have an old 1978 Chevrolet that's just sitting in the garage you can use until you can afford something better, it was my daughter's before she went to college. It's a little rusty and has a dent or two, but you're welcome to use it if you want. Stop by the cashier's office, they have a check ready for you and they'll cash it too."

"Thanks Doc."

Johnathan left the hospital to start a new life. He had no family and knew no one in the small town of Breezewood, but decided he was going to make a new start here. He really didn't want to go back to Virginia where he and his family had lived, it would have been too depressing for him. It was late March and spring was here and he thought, *this was the perfect time to start a new life*.

Chapter Seven

TAKE TIME TO ARGUE

J ohnathan looked the house over and he loved it, and what appealed most to him was the ten-foot privacy fence that circled the property. He walked over to the sliding glass door and looked out at the spacious yard. Hmmm…he thought, *could use some yardwork*. Johnathan looked past the fence and he could see the gray roof of the house on the other side of the weathered fence behind his place. He thought, *yes, this is perfect*.

The car that the doctor had lent him was not much to look at, but it was a ride until he could get something better. He had noticed a hardware store on the way to his new place that had a rusty sign over the door that read, "Ed's Hardware" and he decided to go purchase some garden tools to clean up the yard. He got in the car and headed to the hardware store across town.

The hardware parking lot was small, but Johnathan spied an empty spot and drove just past the empty spot and put the car into reverse to back in. Suddenly a small, white, sports car sped into his spot. He got out of his car and saw a young blonde-haired woman behind the wheel and as he approached her car, she was getting out and Johnathan noticed that she was quite attractive. She was wearing a white blouse, dark red slacks, and black high heels and although he thought, *she was pretty, but that didn't change the fact that she had stolen his parking spot.*

"Didn't you see me getting ready to back into this spot?" he asked.

She looked at him with disdain. "I guess you were just too slow," and she turned to leave.

"You're very rude."

Ellie turned back and looked at Johnathan. "And who are you supposed to be...James Dean?"

"What? No, I'm..."

"That black leather jacket you have on, it's real classy."

Johnathan looked down at his worn jacket. "What's wrong with my jacket?"

Ellie then looked over at his car with an amused look on her face. "How many people died in *that* wreck?"

"It isn't my..."

"You must be one of those hillbillies I've heard tell of. Or are you a serial killer?"

Johnathan was wearing old blue jeans, a faded blue shirt, and his black leather jacket. He looked down at his worn, black boots and grimaced thinking, *This woman was down-right arrogant*, and he felt his face turning red.

"No, I'm not a hillbilly. Who are you, Barbie? Where's Ken? Will he be joining you soon, and is he as rude as you?"

Ellie looked at him with disdain. "Your disgusting, are you homeless? I'm sorry, I can't spare any change."

"I don't want anything from...."

"Excuse me Mr. Hillbilly, I have more important things to do than to chat with a homeless person." Ellie then turned and walked down the sidewalk towards the hardware store to purchase the mouse traps her mother had asked for.

Johnathan watched her walk away and thought, *what a mental case*. He climbed back in his car and looked for another spot. He found one and pulled in thinking, *I better not back up this time because that crazy woman might try to take this spot too*.

He chuckled to himself and muttered, "I guess I do look like a homeless person."

Ellie bought several mouse traps and thanked Ed, and then headed for the door and just as she reached the door, she tripped over the worn welcome mat that had curled up from age and weather. As she fell forward, she put her free hand out towards the door to catch herself just as Johnathan was reaching for the door handle. The force of Ellie's fall pushed the door open quickly and with force, and the door hit Johnathan in the head and knocked him back several steps.

"Are you stalking me?" Ellie demanded.

"No." He rubbed his forehead and he could feel a knot beginning to form and it hurt. "What's wrong with you lady, are you trying to kill me?" he said angrily.

"If you're stalking me I have friends on the Police Force."

"Wow, you actually have friends?" he said sarcastically, still rubbing his head.

Ellie was feeling the side of the door with a concerned look on her face. "I hope your head didn't damage Ed's door."

"What is wrong with you? Did you escape from a mental institute or something?" he said as he continued to stare at her while rubbing his head.

Ellie looked at him and feigned concern. "Oh look, you have a knot on your head. I guess that makes you a knot-headed hillbilly."

"Lady you have real issues. Does your keeper know you're loose?"

Ellie glared at him. "Stop stalking me Mr. Hillbilly!" She turned and walked towards her car.

Johnathan was livid and he yelled after her, "You're a demon! A Demon lady, that's what you are." Then he yelled even louder, "I might be a hillbilly, but you're a Demon lady, and if I know of *anyone* who's stalking you, I'll make sure and warn them what they're in for!"

She smiled with satisfaction as she walked away.

Chapter Eight

ANOTHER STRANGE DREAM

When Ellie arrived at her mother's house she saw her mother standing on the porch.

"What took you so long Ellie? I was beginning to worry."

"I had a run-in with some strange, homeless man. I think he's a drifter or something."

"I worry about you honey, you should find a good man and settle down," Joan said with a worried look on her face.

"I'm fine Mom, just another rude man who thinks he something that he isn't," Ellie said scowling.

"What happened to you Ellie? When you were a young child you were so sweet and kind, and your faith was unstoppable. You've let that divorce destroy you. Did you ever stop to think that maybe he's lonely, or perhaps he's down on his luck?" Joan asked.

"That's not my problem, besides he's very rude and he was dressed like a hobo," she replied.

"Sometimes people just need a smile and a kind word. Have you tried that?"

"He's a man!" Ellie said.

"Oh honey, what am I going to do with you? You love your hate, don't you?" she said as she shook her head.

Maybe she had been too rough on the stranger. She didn't mean to hit him with the door but then again, she felt some satisfaction knowing she got some payback on a man after what they had done to her. Men were nothing but liars and cheaters and you couldn't trust any of them. They were nothing but pigs with shoes.

"I have to go Mom," she said after handing the mouse-traps to her mother.

"Ok hon. Be careful." Joan walked her to the door.

Ellie got in her car and headed home. She was tired because she hadn't gotten much sleep last night due to another one of those crazy dreams. It was hard to go back to sleep after that, and a nap would be great.

Ellie went through the gate of her chain link fence and unlocked the front door and entered the house. She thought about the stranger, *Why was she thinking about him? After all, he was just a bum. He was sort of handsome but somewhat thin, like he couldn't afford a meal. Maybe he was on drugs.*

She changed into her pajamas and set the alarm clock. She didn't want to sleep too late and miss the whole day. It was ten o'clock and she set the alarm for twelve and then she climbed into bed, pulling the sheets over her and telling herself that if she had that dream again, she would try to pay more attention to the surroundings; if she could remember to do that. She got into bed and dozed off and slipped back into the strange dream.

She was back in the vacant house and everything was the same. Belle was there and as usual, Belle went to the glass door and began to whine. The lights were on in the living room and as she looked straight ahead in front of her, she saw two darkened doorways which she assumed were two bedrooms, or perhaps a bedroom and bathroom.

Suddenly, she heard a noise coming from one of the empty rooms and she stared at the doorway directly in front of her, trying to peer into the room through the dark frame of the door. She began to slowly walk towards the doorway when suddenly she froze as a massive dog slowly walked out of the darkened entryway. She could hear its toenails clicking on the wooden floor and the thud of its huge paws with each step it took. The dog stopped just outside of the entryway and stood still, staring at Ellie. She quickly looked over at Belle, and Belle was staring out the glass sliding doors as if she were unaware of the presence of the huge dog. Ellie quickly looked back at the dog and began to scrutinize him and the first thing she noticed was his eyes. They were amber-colored and there was a strange luster to them, but they seemed friendly and Ellie's fear began to loosen its grip on her. The dog was big and muscular, and its fur was gray-black, and it looked like a German Shepherd, but she could see it was mixed with what she guessed to be Wolf.

She finally found her voice. "Hello boy…girl? What are you doing here?" The Wolf-dog stared at her and then he began to whine while looking around the room.

"It's alright boy, come here." She extended her hand towards the strange dog.

The dog turned around and went back into the dark room disappearing from sight. Ellie was not scared any longer because she felt that the dog meant her no harm. Then she heard a man's voice inquiring, "Petey, where are you?" It was a man's voice and it startled her. The voice was gentle, yet sad, and it had a soothing timber to it. She looked around but saw no one in the room.

Ellie was awakened by a loud noise. "What in the world…?" she mumbled. The sound was coming from the back of her house. She went towards the kitchen window to look out into the backyard to see what was going on. *Was someone in her yard?* As she drew close to the window the noise got louder. She pulled the curtain back and peered out the window but saw no one in her yard. It sounded like a chain saw and then she realized that it was coming from the vacant house behind her that belonged to Jack Mosely. Ellie thought to herself, *Maybe Jack figured it was time to clean up that jungle he had going on over there* she thought.

Chapter Nine

NO NEED FOR GROCERIES TODAY

J ohnathan didn't care much for eating out. He preferred home cooking, and he was a good cook and he enjoyed cooking. He was hungry and decided to go to the grocery store in town.

He put his tools away and then looked at the yard with satisfaction. The yard was cleaning up rather well and he only had a few more things to do, and the yard would look like a real yard instead of a jungle. He washed his face and studied his face in the mirror. Well, the Demon lady was right about one thing, he could use a shave and a haircut. Maybe later, first comes food.

He got in his car and drove to the grocery store. He parked his car and walked up to the cart rack and pulled out a cart and entered the store. He got halfway down the aisle and had put several items in his cart when he saw the Demon lady at the other end of the store near the vegetable section. He had images of her running her cart over his heels and breaking his feet. The next image was of the Demon lady running him and his groceries over with her car, leaving him to die in the parking lot amongst his scattered groceries.

He decided that maybe eating out today wasn't such a bad idea. He left the cart where it sat and walked out of the store, occasionally glancing back to see if the Demon woman was chasing him with her deadly grocery cart or trying to run him down with her sports car. He left and drove through a drive-through fast food joint.

Chapter Ten

WATCHING FOR THE DEMON LADY

Johnathan went back to the grocery store an hour later and drove around the parking lot several times looking for the Demon lady's car and not seeing it, he carefully entered the store looking around to make sure she wasn't in site.

After paying for his groceries he went home and put the groceries away and he realized he needed several other items from the hardware store. He drove to the hardware store and parked in front and upon nearing the shop door, he remembered that this was the door that almost knocked him out and he approached it cautiously. He peered through the glass door looking for the Demon lady and saw that it was safe. He opened the door and entered the shop.

"Hello young man, forget something?"

"Yes, I need a weed-eater."

"We have several, take your pick," Ed told him, pointing to the back of the store.

Johnathan selected a green and yellow one and grabbed some string, and then took them up front to the counter.

"You new in town?" Ed asked.

"Yes, I am."

"Have you been to our park yet?" Ed inquired.

"No sir, I haven't."

"We have a mighty pretty park down by the river. Has ducks and other critters and it's a nice place to picnic, or just relax on the bench and feed the ducks."

Johnathan thought, *that sounded like a great idea*. "That sounds wonderful, I could use some down time." It seemed he had been busy since he had left the hospital and a break would be nice, just relaxing in the warm sun feeding the ducks. After all, the Doctor had said to take it easy.

"Got some feed for the ducks if you care to feed them."

"Sure, why not."

"Just be careful down by the river, the dam isn't far from the park and it's a dangerous spot. You go over that dam and no one will ever see you again. The dam has a whirlpool and a strong undertow and there are signs posted that say, no swimming. Nobody swims there."

"Thanks for the info."

Johnathan paid for the weed-eater and string, but Ed refused the money for the feed. "Feed is on the house."

Johnathan thanked him and walked back to his car looking up at the sky and thinking, what a perfect day to be lazy. He guessed the temperature to be about seventy degrees. The sun was shining brightly, and it felt warm on his face. There were several white, puffy clouds that looked like cotton balls hanging perfectly still against the blue sky. He heard a flock of geese honking above him and shading his eyes with his hand, he looked up at them as they flew by overhead.

He took off his jacket and put it in the car along with the items he had purchased. Johnathan decided to relax in the park and then afterward, he would visit the barber shop and get cleaned up. He also planned to find a store in town and buy some new clothes. He hadn't really thought about cleaning up due to his depression from the loss of his family and Petey, but he decided it was time to get back into life again. He then began to think of his family and Petey and he became melancholy. He pushed the thoughts out of his mind and told himself he was going to have a good day without any negative thoughts.

When Johnathan pulled into the parking lot by the river he noticed that the water was not very wide at this spot. He spotted a green park bench on a small hill close to the water and he could see that the dam was not far from where he was and he thought, *that's odd, this place looks like the same place I saw in my dream while in the hospital.* He walked over to the edge of the hill where he could see a tow path that was slightly hidden by the hill. The path was about twenty yards below the hill, and he saw several people walking along the path. He went back and sat down on the bench stretching his legs out in front of him and crossing his feet.

When he opened the bag of feed, the ducks seemed to know what Johnathan had in the bag. The ducks began to gather around him, quacking and flapping their wings causing several small, wispy, white feathers to rise up and slowly float to the ground. Johnathan threw some feed out on the grass and as it scattered, he watched the ducks devour the feed. Several of them began to argue with each other over the seed but settled down quickly when Johnathan threw another handful of seed to them. He looked up at the sun and closed his eyes and he could feel the sun warming his body and thought, *A man could fall asleep here. Now this was living!*

After a while, Johnathan dozed off. In his dream, he was back in Iraq with Sneaky Pete. He saw the man with his arm cocked back in preparation to throw the explosive at him and then he saw Petey running towards the man. He could see the man's face, and everything seemed as though it was in slow motion. Suddenly he heard screaming from somewhere and realized he had fallen asleep and the screams had jolted him awake. He realized the screaming was emanating from down below the hill towards the river, and it was a woman's scream.

Chapter Eleven

SAVING A BEAUTIFUL SPIRIT

Ellie usually went to the park on weekends to walk the tow path. It was a beautiful day and she had decided to walk to the park, as it was not far from her house. As she walked down the tow path she observed the tiny, green leaves and the small pink and white blossoms sprouting from the branches of the ornamental trees. The grass had already turned green and soon summer would be here. It was a perfect spring day and she was happy to be out in the fresh air. The birds were tweeting and singing, flying from place to place busily building their nests and she saw two gray squirrels run down a tree, one chasing the other.

The tow path ran parallel to the river and as Ellie was walking and enjoying the wildlife she looked out towards the river and she saw something in the water, and it took her a second to realize what it was. She put her hand to her chest and said, "oh my God!" There was a small yellow-golden colored dog swimming frantically up-river and although he was swimming as hard as he could, the current was slowing taking him down-river towards the dam. Ellie knew that if the dog went over the dam he would drown for sure.

She began to scream for help. "Somebody, help! Help me, please! There's a dog drowning in the river!" She looked around but she didn't see anyone. "Please someone help! There's a dog in the river and he's going to drown!" What could she do? If she jumped in the water she knew she would be swept over the dam with the poor dog. She thought of Belle and began to scream louder looking around for some-body to help the little dog before he went over the dam. "Oh God, please send someone to help that poor dog or he will drown!" she mumbled to herself as she watched the dog drift closer to the dam and then she began to scream again

When Johnathan gathered his wits, he stood up and ran to the edge of the hill and looked down at the tow path. *My God, it's the Demon lady! Why is she screaming?* Then he saw the dog and realized he was headed for the dam. Without hesita-tion he ripped his boots off and ran to the river and dove in, swimming as fast as he could towards the dog.

The current was strong, and it helped him reach the dog quickly and when he finally reached the dog, he grabbed him by the scruff of the neck and began swimming towards the shore with his free arm. The water was taking them down-river fast and he prayed that he would be able to reach the shore before they both went over the dam. He remembered what the man Ed had told him at the hardware store, *"you go over that dam, and no one will ever see you again."* This spurred him on, and he swam faster.

He could hear the Demon lady yelling. "Hurry, you're going to go over the dam!" He swam harder and he felt his strength begin to weaken. Lying in the hospital bed those months had weakened him and he was beginning to feel it. He didn't think he was going to make it and he wasn't far from the drop off point. He thought, *No, I'm not going to die like this, not after all I've been through.* And then he envisioned what the newspaper headlines would read: "WAR HERO DROWNS AS DEMON LADY CHEERS."

He could still hear the Demon lady yelling. "Hurry! You'll both drown if you go over the dam!"

His adrenaline kicked in and he pushed harder. The dam was only a few feet away and he spotted a tree root that was sticking out past the bank into the water. As the current pushed him sideways he grabbed onto the root, praying that it would hold him. He grabbed the root and he and the dog stopped with the dam only a few feet away. The current was very strong near the dam and he held on for dear life.

Ellie had run down to the riverbank over to where Johnathan was clinging to the tree root. "Hand me the dog!" she shouted, extending her hands towards him. With one hand holding the tree root, he lifted the dog up and out of the water to Ellie and she grabbed the dog and held it to her chest. Johnathan was struggling to get out of the water, but the bank was slippery and as he was slowly inching his way out of the water, he slipped and almost lost his hold on the branch. He began to climb again when he felt someone grab his long hair and begin to pull him upward. It was painful and he screamed.

"Yeowwww... let go of my hair! Stop! You're pulling my hair out!" Ellie ignored him and continued to pull him up until he was on shore before she let go.

Johnathan rolled over on his back soaking wet and breathing heavily, and when he looked up he saw the Demon lady looking at him and holding the dog. She then turned and began to walk up the hill.

"Hey, wait a minute! Where are you go...?" He had swallowed some water and he began choking, causing him to have a coughing fit in the middle of his sentence. Ellie ignored him and continued to walk up the hill with the dog in her arms holding him like a baby.

"Hey, I'm talking to you!" he shouted. He got to his feet and began to climb up the hill after her, almost falling twice before he reached her. He ran in front of her blocking her path and she stopped.

Ellie tried to move around him, and he moved with her, blocking her way.

"Excuse me Mr. Hillbilly. Please move."

"That's my dog!"

"Your dog!?" Ellie exclaimed.

"Yea, that's right. I saved his life and that makes him mine."

"Well if I hadn't of yelled you wouldn't have been there to save him, now would you? And besides, I know he's a stray because I've seen him around town for the past several days and I've tried to catch him, but he always runs away. Now I have him and I'm afraid that makes him mine."

"You think your yelling and screaming got him out of the water? I'm the one who jumped into the freezing water and saved him," he said, finally catching his breath.

"Well, I'm sorry Mr. Hillbilly but possession is nine-tenths of the law and as you can see, I have him in my possession. He's in *my* arms not yours!" she said smugly.

Johnathan was trying to control his temper. "He's mine because I saved his life and by the way, do you always go around torturing people who are new to this town? You should be wearing a hazardous warning sign that says: Caution! Demon lady: Stay back 100 feet."

Her mouth dropped open. "Aren't you ungrateful!"

"What?"

"I pulled you out of the river and saved your life!"

"You didn't save my life! I was doing fine until you pulled my hair." *The nerve of her,* he thought.

Ellie threw her head back and laughed. "You couldn't beat your way out of a wet paper bag. Look at you, your skin and bones! You're just lucky I was there to save you. You need to go eat something and gain some weight. Are you on drugs or something?"

"Lucky? I didn't need any help from you. You're crazy! Are you off your meds, or did you escape from a mental institute?" Johnathan asked. He was getting madder by the moment and thinking to himself, *this woman is a nut-cake*.

The dog looked at them both and thought, *I like them both but why are they growling at each other? Why can't they just sniff each other and be friends? That's what us dogs do, but he knew that humans liked to put their faces together and make smacking noises, but these two humans weren't doing either. He knew from his experience of being around humans that they weren't very smart,* and he thought, *I'll fix this*.

He had been abandoned two weeks ago and had been on his own ever since. He was a Carin Terrier and his fur was a solid gold-yellow color and when the sun hit his back, the fur on his back appeared to have a reddish tint to it. His ears were long and his big, round, black eyes and black-button nose stood out in contrast to his yellow fur, and he had been mistaken for a fox by several people in town.

Ellie's face turned red and she was about to say something when the dog began to struggle in her arms. The dog struggled so much that she had to bend down and release him before he jumped out of her arms and fell.

"Hey! Come back here boy!" Ellie clapped her hands together.

He ran over to Johnathan and jumped up on Johnathan's leg and Johnathan picked him up.

"Well, I guess he wants me. He knows a demon when he sees one and it looks to me like I have possession of him now. What was that you said about possession being nine-tenths of the law?" Johnathan said laughing.

Ellie glared at him. "He's mine. Give him back."

The dog began to struggle again, and Johnathan had to set him down. The dog ran back to Ellie and she picked him up. "That's right Fluffy, come to Mommy."

"Fluffy?" Johnathan exclaimed. "He's a boy, not a sissy. I'm going to name him Petey."

"I don't think so, he's coming with me," Ellie said smugly and laughed. As she started to turn and walk away the dog began struggling again and she had to set him back down. The dog ran back to Jonathan and he picked him up. "Well now, he's with his Daddy and he's happy. See, he's wagging his tale. We'll see you later."

The dog began struggling again and Johnathan had to set him down and the dog ran a few feet away, positioning himself off to the side between them both and sat down and looked from Ellie to Johnathan, continuing to look from one to the other thinking to himself, *Don't they know what I'm trying to tell them?*

"Apparently he doesn't want either of us," Ellie said.

"Don't you see? He's trying to tell us that he likes us both, you just don't understand dog language," Johnathan said in disgust.

"Well, as much as I hate to admit it, maybe that hillbilly brain of yours does work somewhat."

"What is your problem lady? I am NOT a hillbilly!" Johnathan said through gritted teeth.

She just glowered at him and crossed her arms.

"I have an idea," he said.

"Oh no, he's thinking again!" Ellie replied sarcastically, throwing her arms up in the air.

"Why don't we share him?" Johnathan asked.

"What? That's a really stupid idea." Ellie rolled her eyes and crossed her arms again.

"No, it isn't. It could be kind of like a child custody thing in a divorce."

"Divorce? Ha! Why I wouldn't marry you if you were the last man on earth!"

"Well, if I was the last man on earth I'd be too busy to fool with you, believe me," he said laughing.

"Oh, you're a regular comedian aren't you?" Ellie retorted.

"Do you have any other ideas? Because if we don't help him he'll end up in the pound or worse yet, he could be killed."

She hesitated. "No, I don't. But that's impossible to do, it just won't work."

"No, it isn't impossible and yes it can work. I'll take him one week and you can have him the next week, and we can alternate weeks."

"That's ridiculous, how is that going to work? That means I'll have to look at your ugly face once a week and I'm certainly not going to tell you where I live. You can forget that idea," she said in disgust.

"We could meet here in the park every Saturday or Sunday and make the switch, and you could wear a bag over your head, so you won't have to look at my ugly face. Maybe the town will get lucky and you'll suffocate yourself, then Petey will be all mine! That sounds wonderful to me," he said with a big smile on his face.

"You're disgusting."

Johnathan smiled. "Well what do you think?" he asked.

Ellie thought about it. "Ok fine. But I get him first."

"Give me your phone number in case you don't show up next week."

"Yea…that's *not* going to happen. I'll be here next Sunday at noon with the dog."

"Let me give you my phone number in case something happens."

She rolled her eyes and said, "I don't want your phone number."

Johnathan breathed out heavily in exasperation. "Quit being hard-headed and just take it please, for the dog's sake. It won't hurt you to take it and you don't have to use it if you don't want to." He had a pen and he wrote down his number on the receipt from the hardware store.

"Well, alright if you insist." Ellie thought she would patronize him so she could leave with the dog, planning to

SAVING A BEAUTIFUL SPIRIT

throw his number away later. She took the paper and stuffed it in her pocket.

Johnathan frowned. "I don't like the name you picked, and you don't like mine. We need to think of a name before you go."

A young girl was walking by and she heard them talking and she said, "why don't you name him Jasper, it's such a pretty name."

Johnathan and Ellie looked at each other.

"Sounds good to me," Johnathan said.

Ellie breathed a heavy sigh. "Fine."

She called the dog. "Come on Jasper, come to Momma." The dog ran over to her and she picked him up and the dog licked her face several times. "I guess he's ok with the arrangement. See you Sunday at noon right here and don't be late, or you'll have to forfeit your turn. Goodbye Hillbilly man." She turned and began to walk home.

"See you next Sunday, Demon lady!" he hollered.

Jasper was looking around at Johnathan and thought, *These two humans forgot to sniff each other or make smacking sounds, but at least they understood my message.*

Little did Hillbilly man know that Ellie had no intentions of being anywhere near the park next Sunday. It was her dog now and the thought of sharing the dog was the most ridiculous idea she'd ever heard of and for all she knew, Hillbilly man could be a serial killer.

She looked down at Jasper and said in a high-pitched child's voice, "aww…you're my baby now Jasper. You're sooo cute! We'll go to my house and I'll give you a bath and a nice meal." She liked the name Jasper, it fit him perfectly. She thought of the name he wanted to name the dog; *Petey*. *Now where had she heard that name before?*

Chapter Twelve

JASPER HAS OTHER PLANS

J asper had other plans for his two new humans that he had
adopted. He had been on his own enough to know his way
around the small town and he knew where everyone lived.
He knew that these two humans called Ellie and Johnathan
lived near each other and he was sure they weren't aware of
it. He knew that there was a hole in the fence hidden behind
the bushes that separated their backyards because he had
used it before, and he had also seen them both through the
windows of their houses. Each house was about forty yards
from the tall fence. Jasper thought, *Perfect! All he had to do*
now was look cute, and act innocent until next Sunday and
then he would execute plan B.

Ellie ran some warm water in the tub. The weather was
warm, but she knew that the river water was still cold, and
Jasper was shaking. She wrapped him in a towel until the
bath-water was ready. She still had some dog shampoo and

many of the other dog items that she had kept after Belle had passed. She washed Jasper and dried him off with a fresh blue towel and then she put some canned dog food in Belle's old bowl and drew some cold water from the tap into another bowl. She placed the bowls on the floor and Jasper ate the food and drank most of the water and then licking his lips, he laid down in Belle's old bed which was more than enough room. Ellie laughed at how small Jasper looked in Belle's huge bed. Jasper went to sleep, and he was happy. He didn't have just one house now...he had two.

Chapter Thirteen

JASPER PLAYS BOTH SIDES

Ellie let Jasper out in the yard later in the afternoon. Her yard was surrounded by a chain link fence except for the back where the wooden fence was. She sat on the porch and watched Jasper explore the yard. She could hear the humming of a weed-eater coming from the vacant house behind her. She assumed Jack was still cleaning up his yard and she wondered why. *Was he planning to rent again?* She hoped not, but the long backyards of each house gave her plenty of room and privacy, and she was happy about that.

Jasper ran around the yard sniffing everything and he seemed to be enjoying the yard. As Ellie watched Jasper, her thoughts turned to the stranger. *What was his story? Where did he come from? Maybe he wasn't as bad as she thought.* She laughed thinking about what he said about being the last man on earth and then caught herself, *she hadn't really laughed in almost three years*. He did have a sense of humor and he did risk his life for Jasper, which showed some type of loyalty and commitment. She probably shouldn't have pulled him up by his hair, but she didn't want him to drown, he looked very weak. She could have grabbed his shirt, but it was more fun pulling him up by his hair. Apparently he wasn't in particularly good shape which was a shame for a man as good looking as him to let himself go like that. Maybe he was on drugs. That was a scary thought, a drug addict running around Breezewood.

Jasper came up to her and licked her hand. "Hi Jasper, do you like your new home? Don't worry, you won't have to go stay with that man. He probably lives behind a garbage dumpster. I'm going to keep you here with me."

That's what you think, Jasper thought. *I'll have you two together soon enough, and then I'll have a family of my own.*

Ellie thought about going to church again and then thought, *Why? God doesn't care about her, or anything about her. Maybe she would go one Sunday just to shut her mother up.* Her thoughts kept going back to the stranger. She couldn't seem to shake him from her mind. *What was it about him? She had promised herself that she was not getting into another relationship, so why was she even thinking about that? She was sure that he was just like all the other men that had treated her so badly.* She pushed the thoughts of the stranger out of her mind and took Jasper back in the house.

Johnathan finished with the yardwork and went back in the house to make lunch. He made a peanut butter and jelly sandwich and drank down a glass of cold milk. He thought about the Demon lady, *Why was she so hateful? She was so beautiful, but so nasty. Did something happen to her to make her so hateful? Why was he even letting her rent space in his head? Forget her! She had better show up at the park next week!* But he didn't trust her to be there like they had agreed.

The Demon lady was right, he was out of shape and he planned on buying some hand weights as soon as he had the time. He thought of Jasper and he couldn't wait until Sunday when he would get Jasper for a whole week. He thought of Petey and wondered if he would be mad at him for bonding with another dog. He thought, *Of course not, Petey would be proud of him for sharing his love with another dog.*

He decided to go talk with Pastor Bennett, and he left the house and drove to the church. The Pastor was in and he welcomed Johnathan into his office.

"Hello John, how are you?"

"I'm doing well, Bill."

"What brings you here?"

"Just wanted to talk."

"Sure John, is there anything special you need to talk about?"

"Well…you may think this is stupid."

"Try me."

"Do you think animals go to Heaven?" he said hesitantly.

"That is not a stupid question John. Many people ask me that because people love their pets and the Bible tells us that

God's love cannot be measured or weighed, and that it is unfathomable and unlimited, and for anyone to say differently is limiting the love of God, don't you think?"

"Yea, I never thought of that. Thanks, you make a valid point and I believe you. Do you think Sneaky Pete would be mad at me, or jealous if I adopted and loved another dog?"

"Certainly not John, he would be proud of you for loving and caring for another of his kind, and so would God."

"That's what I thought, but I wanted the opinion from a man of God."

"Your dog is waiting for you in glory land and enjoying himself like you can't even imagine."

"Thanks Bill, that makes me feel much better."

Bill looked at him intently and asked, "have you adopted another dog? Maybe that's just what the doctor ordered, and I should know, I'm a doctor." They both laughed at his joke. The Doctor was well aware of the therapeutic value of owning a pet.

"I'm thinking about it."

"Great! So, how do you like our little town of Breezewood?"

"It's great, and everyone here is very nice and friendly." He hesitated and then said, "except there was one person I met that was a little strange."

"Who are you talking about, crazy Emma down at the grocery store?"

"No. Never mind, it's nothing."

"Tell me about it, I can see it's bothering you. What you say here, stays here."

John looked around the office and then he gazed out the window thinking of the Demon lady. "This person is a very miserable person and I guess they just want everyone else to be miserable too," he answered.

Bill leaned back in his chair crossing his legs and clasping his hands together. "You know sometimes John we just don't know how a person feels or what they have gone through, until we have walked in their shoes. Some people can't handle stress and hardship like you can, and people like us have God to lean on, but they don't."

John sighed. "You're right Bill. I guess I need to work on my patience."

"And mercy and forgiveness," Bill added with a smile.

Pastor Bennett knew exactly who John was talking about. He knew Ellie, and he had come to know John. He knew they were both hurting and lonely, and that they both had a chip on their shoulder. That's why he had talked his friend Jack into renting his house to John. He had felt God pushing him to do this and he thought that maybe Ellie and John could get together and that it would be beneficial for both of them. And so, he moved John into the house behind Ellie's and prayed, letting God handle the rest.

Johnathan got up from his chair. "I just wanted to know mostly about what you thought about Petey. Thank you Bill, you've taken a load off my mind, I guess I should let you get back to business."

"No problem John, anytime. Are you going to adopt?"

"Yes, I think I will. As soon as I find the right dog." Johnathan said staring out the window and thinking of Jasper and the Demon woman. He had a smile on his face.

Chapter Fourteen

JASPER ONLY ESCAPES
ON SUNDAYS

S unday finally arrived and Johnathan walked to the park to wait for Jasper and the Demon lady. He arrived fifteen minutes early and decided to feed the ducks and enjoy the warm sun on his face. Something told him she would not show up, and after a while he looked at his watch and it read ten after twelve. Either she was late, she didn't plan on showing up, or maybe something happened to prevent her from coming. He waited a little while longer giving her the benefit of the doubt, but he was sure that she had no plans to hand Jasper over to him.

A little while later he looked at his watch again and it was a little past twelve thirty; she was a no show. She lied. He knew that she was keeping Jasper for herself and it hurt Johnathan knowing that he couldn't see Jasper. He had fallen in love with Jasper and wanted to take care of him and he felt as though God had led him to save Jasper's life and besides, he was lonely, and he wanted a friend. He began to get angry and thought, *That Demon lady! Wait till I see her again.* Then he thought, *Do I really want to see her again?* Yes, he did, but only because of Jasper. He was a cute little thing and Johnathan had liked him from the start. Maybe because he had lost Petey, or perhaps because he had saved the dog's life, like Petey had saved his. Johnathan was sad and angry at the same time. People! He decided to go home and get away from people for now. He was disappointed but before he left, he said a prayer and then he headed home.

Jasper knew his week with Ellie was up and it was time to go to Johnathan's house. When Jasper cried at the back door, Ellie let Jasper out and then she went back inside to wash dishes where she could keep an eye on Jasper through the kitchen window. She watched him walk around sniffing the bushes and flowers and enjoying the spacious yard. Satisfied that Jasper was ok, she began to wash dishes glancing occasionally out the window to check on Jasper.

As Jasper got closer to the bushes where the hidden hole in the fence was, he looked up at the kitchen window and as soon as Ellie moved off to the side away from the window, he quickly ran in between the bushes and through the small hole in the wooden fence. He ran through Johnathan's yard and peered inside the glass doors, but he didn't see Johnathan inside, so he went around front and laid on the front porch and waited for him to come home.

When Johnathan turned the corner and went through the open gates of the fence he saw Jasper sitting on the front porch. "Jasper! What are you doing, how did you get here?" Jasper stood up and wagged his tale as Johnathan approached him. He ran off the porch and jumped into Johnathan's arms and Johnathan hugged him. "How did you get here boy? Never mind, I'm just glad you're here." So, he thought, *Jasper had escaped the Demon lady and came right to him. I knew he was my dog!* He took Jasper inside and shut the door.

Ellie looked out the window to check on Jasper, but she didn't see him anywhere and she thought that maybe he had gone around the side of the house. She took off her lemon-colored apron and went out the door looking around the yard calling Jasper's name. She went around the side of the house and then she circled the house, but Jasper was nowhere to be seen and she began to panic. *How did he get out!? Did he dig a hole under the chain link fence, or did he jump over the fence? Oh my God, he could be anywhere or possibly hurt.* Then she froze in fear and thought, *What if he is down by the dam again?* Her mind was moving at the speed of light. *What should I do?* She thought of Belle and she felt weak with fear and was unsure what she should do. *Should she call the stranger? No, that was out of the question, he would call her irresponsible and she would look foolish and he would want Jasper, claiming that he was the more responsible one. Hadn't she acted like she was the most responsible? Yes, she had but still...there was really no one else to call. Did she throw his number away? No, it was in the pocket of her white slacks and they were in the washer. Had she washed them? Oh God, please let me find Jasper and let him be alright,* she thought as she hurried to look for her slacks.

She found the crumpled paper in the pocket of her pants and she unfolded it and started to punch the number in her phone. She hesitated for a moment. *Should she call him? He would berate her and if he did, she would have to take it.* She finished punching the number in and the phone began to ring. *How humiliating!*

Johnathan's phone rang and he picked it up thinking, *Who was calling him?* He didn't know anyone and then it hit him, Jasper was here, and he had given the Demon lady his number, so it had to be her. He smiled and thought, *Oh boy, I'm going to play her like a fiddle. Payback at last!*

He pushed the talk button. "Hello." At first there was only silence, then he repeated his greeting. "Hello." He was smiling.

Ellie took a deep breath. "I wouldn't have called you, but Jasper has gotten loose. I don't know how, but he got away and I need your help. I'm worried sick."

"I thought you were the responsible one. Did you forget? I'm just a dumb hillbilly." He had to hold the phone away while he laughed quietly.

"I don't know how he got loose but please, let's don't argue. What's important right now is finding Jasper."

"You lied to me. I waited in the park for an hour and if you hadn't of lied and kept your end of the bargain, Jasper would be with me safe and sound."

"I…I know," she said sniffling.

Johnathan could tell she was crying, and he felt sorry for her. *What was wrong with him?* He was starting to feel sorry for her when he should be happy. He couldn't torture her anymore.

"It's ok, he's here with me."

"You kidnapped him!? You're reprehensible!" she said in an angry voice.

I knew it! She was a Demon lady with a capital D, he thought. "I did not kidnap him. He was here on my porch when I came back from the park where YOU were supposed to meet me! So technically, you kidnapped him from me and besides, I don't even know where you live, how could I take him?"

Ellie knew he was right. "Look, I'm just glad he's safe," and she hung up the phone and threw it on the couch. Ellie was completely humiliated.

Johnathan thought, *I got her!* But he wasn't feeling as good about it as he thought he would.

Chapter Fifteen

THE DREAMER GETS DREAMED

E llie walked over and plopped down on the couch, she was
so tired and disgusted that she laid down and fell asleep.
She was back in the dream again, only this time it was more
progressed. She was in the vacant house and Belle was at her
usual place looking out the sliding glass door with her ears
standing straight in the air and whining. Ellie looked over at
the dark silhouette of the bedroom doorway and sure enough
the Wolf-dog appeared. She and the dog stared at each other
for several seconds and then Ellie spoke. "Hello boy, what's
your name?" His amber-colored eyes looked lonely and they
had a certain sadness to them, and she felt an instant bond
with him. The dog whined and he began to pant with his pink
tongue extending out of his mouth, looking over at the couch
and then back to Ellie. The dog's tongue retracted back into
his mouth and his ears went up and he whined again. He
slowly began to walk towards Ellie, and she became a little

fearful, but she knew she was dreaming, and the fear disappeared. The dog stopped about two feet from Ellie and his ears relaxed, as though he sensed her fear and stopped to let her know he wouldn't hurt her.

Suddenly, she heard the same gentle voice that she had heard in her last dream. "Hello." She quickly looked over to her left at the couch and gasped. The Hillbilly man was sitting on the couch smiling at her. It was a friendly smile, and then he spoke. "Go ahead and pet him, he won't bite you." Ellie stared at Johnathan and his scars were red and she realized that his wounds were fresh, and the scars had a small amount of blood on them. The Wolf-dog looked over at the Hillbilly man and whined, then he slowly began to walk towards Ellie closing the distance between them. She quickly looked back at the dog when she heard him moving closer to her and by that time, the dog was sniffing her leg, and then he sniffed her hand. She could feel its warm breath on her hand, and then he began to lick her hand. She knew this was a dream, but it was so vivid and so real! And she knew that she should be scared, but she wasn't.

"He likes you."

She looked back at the stranger and then she slowly turned her attention back to the Wolf-dog. Carefully, she reached out and began to pet the dog. She could feel its soft, warm fur and it was so real that she gasped. She then looked over at the stranger and he had disappeared and when she looked back at the dog, he was gone too.

Ellie woke up and looked at the clock. It was six o'clock. She pondered her dream and wondered what it meant. *Why was the stranger in her dream?* For some reason she felt rested and relaxed when she should have been frightened and exhausted.

Chapter Sixteen

JASPER EXECUTES PLAN B

J asper knew it was Sunday and it was time to switch houses. He looked to see if Johnathan was looking and not seeing him anywhere, he snuck through the hole in the fence and ran to Ellie's back door and sat on the concrete porch and began to whine at the door, waiting for her to come out.

Ellie was in the kitchen sitting at the table eating lunch when she heard a whining noise and went to the back door, and there sat Jasper! She opened the door and Jasper trotted in like he owned the place. "Welcome home baby," Ellie said with a big smile. She picked Jasper up and gave him a big kiss and a hug and Jasper licked Ellie in return. "How did you get here?"

Jasper looked at her and whined thinking, *call Johnathan and let him know where I am*. And then he thought, *I'm going to get these two together this time*.

Ellie picked up the phone to call the stranger and then she hesitated thinking, *Should she rub it in? After all, now he had lost Jasper…but so had she. No, I'll just call and tell him Jasper is here, so he won't worry.* He may be a hillbilly, but she knew he cared about Jasper, so she decided to call and tell him Jasper was here and then hang up. That way she wouldn't have to converse with him any longer than necessary. She punched in the number.

It was Sunday and Johnathan looked at the clock, it was eleven-thirty and he had to take Jasper to the park soon to make the switch. He had let Jasper out to use the bathroom when he had cried to go out. He went out back to get Jasper, but he was nowhere to be found. *Where did he go?* He looked everywhere and thought he must have gone out the front gate. Johnathan was worried and upset, *I should have closed the gate, what was I thinking?* Johnathan looked all over the yard again and then he searched out in front of the house. He then looked on each side of the house and after a thorough search outside, he went back in the house and looked everywhere, but no Jasper. He was worried sick and thinking the worst he grabbed his jacket and decided to drive around to look for him. He was going to be late for their meeting in the park. *What was he going to tell the Demon lady?* As he was about to leave to look for Jasper the phone rang, and he knew it had to be the Demon lady. He decided not to tell her about Jasper until he had searched for him a little longer. *But what excuse could he give her? That meant he would have to lie, and hadn't he called her a liar?* No, he couldn't lie to her. He stared at the phone for several seconds. *What would he tell her?* He took a deep breath, and then he answered the phone. "Hello."

"Hello Mr. Hillbilly, I just wanted to let you know Jasper is here with me, it seems as though you let him get loose."

"Oh, thank God. I was worried to death!" Johnathan ran his hand over the top of his head, smoothing his hair back. "He just disappeared, and I've been searching for him everywhere. I let him out to use the bathroom and he disappeared. I was just on my way to the park to meet you. I'm sorry."

"Well…it's ok, he's here with me. It seems as though he knows the schedule."

"How does he know when and where to go?"

"I don't know. Our dog is a very smart pooch."

"Excuse me, did you say *our* dog?"

"Did I? I meant *my* dog." She had to smile.

"Did I hear a smile?"

"I don't think so," she retorted, and the smile quickly left her face. *How did he know she was smiling? No, he couldn't know.* Most likely he was trying to flirt with her like all men, but it wasn't going to work. She wasn't the naive young girl she used to be, and she had learned her lesson about men the hard way.

"I was thinking, shouldn't we take him to the veterinarian to get shots?" Jonathan asked.

"You were thinking? I hope you didn't hurt yourself."

"I'm serious. Shouldn't one of us take him to the veterinarian and get his shots up-to-date?"

"Yes, he does need shots. I just haven't had the time to take him. Some people actually have a job."

"I'll take him next week when he decides to come and see me."

"Ok. And while you're there, you should get your shots up-to-date too," Ellie said smiling. *If nothing else, he was entertaining*, she thought.

"Can we just call a truce? What's your name anyway?" Johnathan asked.

"Let's just keep it the way it is. It's bad enough we're connected because of Jasper."

"No truce?" he pleaded.

"We can be civil when it comes to Jasper, but that's it." Ellie hung up the phone. She wasn't rude, just firm.

Johnathan smiled after he hung up. Her insults had made him mad at first, but now they were kind of funny...*get my shots too!* That was funny, and he threw his head back and laughed. Then he thought, *I haven't laughed that hard in a long time.*

For the next five weeks Jasper went back and forth from house to house undetected. They had no idea how Jasper knew where they lived or where to go, but they accepted it which saved them time from having to meet in the park. They had become used to Jasper showing up at each other's house every Sunday, as if he knew what he was doing. It had now become part of the weekly routine. Ellie and Johnathan would call each other to let the other know that Jasper was with them, so the other would not worry about Jasper's disappearance.

Jasper knew humans were stupid, but these two humans seemed to be a little bit slower than most, but he wasn't about to give up. He loved them both and wanted all three of them to be together as a pack. *They had saved his life when others had abandoned him.*

Chapter Seventeen

THE DEMON LADY AND MR. HILLBILLY GO TO CHURCH

Johnathan planned on going to church on Sunday and he decided it was time to get cleaned up. He went to the barber and got a haircut and a shave, and then he went to the only clothing store in town and bought several nice suits, some casual clothes, and several pairs of new shoes.

On Sunday he arrived at the church just in time and he had to go to the restroom before the service started. When he was finished, he rushed out of the bathroom and as he turned the corner he ran into Ellie who was also in hurry to go freshen up her make-up. Johnathan had to grab her by the arms to keep them from running into each other. "You!" Ellie said, "get your hands off me!"

"I'm sorry," he said sheepishly.

"What are you doing here?" she demanded.

"Same thing you are I guess."

"Just keep your distance," she said.

"I will, don't worry. I figure I should stand near the fire alarm in case your presence starts a fire," he said with a big smile.

"You're real funny, aren't you? A real clown. Are you going to juggle your pea-sized brain for us today?" she retorted. "Excuse me." She then hurriedly walked around him and went up front to sit with her mother.

Johnathan sat near the back so he could leave quickly when the service was over. They sang three songs from the hymnal and afterwards the Pastor directed them to sit down. He began preaching about other people's feelings and how people should be kind to each other, and how people should try to walk in other people's shoes before judging them.

Once during the service, Johnathan looked over at Ellie and caught her giving him a side glance, but she quickly looked forward. There was an older lady sitting with her, and he knew it was her mother because the Demon lady looked just like her.

Ellie was shocked seeing the stranger clean shaven and in a suit. After the service Ellie walked over to Pastor Bill and asked, "who is that man over there? Is he a transient?"

"What man?" Bill said looking out over the congregation.

"The one in the dark blue suit and yellow tie."

Johnathan had on a dark blue suit, a light blue shirt, and a butterscotch-colored tie. His tan face was clean shaven, his hair was cut short, and his scars were now clearly visible, and she thought the scars made him look very manly. She thought to herself that he looked rather handsome all cleaned up, and she also noticed that he had put on a little weight.

Bill smiled. "Oh, that's Johnathan Slade. He's a war hero. He lost his wife and two daughters several years ago and he recently lost his dog in Iraq. He's been awarded several medals and his dog was awarded a Silver Cross for saving John's life."

"A war hero? Oh, I wasn't aware of that." She felt ashamed of her behavior when she heard this. Seeing him in a suit and knowing he was a veteran, shocked her. He had lost his family and his dog and was probably all alone in the world. *How wrong she had been!* she thought. And now, she was embarrassed to even look at him.

Ellie was perplexed. " What was his dog doing in Iraq?" she asked.

"John was a demolitions expert and the dog was his partner. Petey's job was to find the explosives and Johnathan's job was to disarm and dispose of them. John saved many lives doing this, but on his last mission he took some shrapnel and his back was broken and that's when he lost his dog. The dog died saving John's life. We weren't sure if he would walk again, but the operation was a success. I don't mean to brag, but I performed the operation. Yes mam, that is one tough determined man. Nothing can stop him."

"Was his dog part Wolf?"

"I don't know, why don't you ask him?"

Ellie felt like a fool. She had treated him so horribly and now she felt two feet tall. *How could she ever face him again? She couldn't ever look him in the face again.* All this time she was thinking that he was nothing but a bum. And now she had found out that he was a veteran with medals and had lost both his family, and his dog.

Johnathan was trying to get out of the church as fast as he could but the woman who was sitting with Ellie approached him before he could get through the crowd that had gathered at the exit. Joan quickly approached Johnathan. "Hello, you must be new in town."

Johnathan grinned sheepishly. "Yes, I'm afraid I am."

"How do you like our town?"

"I like it very much. I've always been partial to small towns."

"Have you met many people?"

"Not really. Only a few people."

"Have you met Ellie, my daughter?" and she pointed towards Ellie.

"Yes, I believe I've seen her around."

"She's single you know."

"I can't imagine why," he said smiling and thinking, who would want to marry the Demon lady?

"What?" Joan asked.

"Ah…I mean, you'd think a woman as beautiful as your daughter would have been married by now."

"She was, but her husband ran off with some fancy woman from New York and she went through a nasty divorce. I never did trust that man and I warned Ellie, but you know how children are; they never listen to their parents no matter how old they are because they know it all. And not over a year ago she dated another loser which I warned her about, and he cheated on her too, and then her dog passed. Ellie's father died with cancer when she was only ten years old and it was very hard on her. She's had a rough time of it, poor dear. She's really a sweet and wonderful girl."

"I'm sorry to hear that." Johnathan remembered what Pastor Bill had said about walking in someone else's shoes. He felt bad for Ellie and felt even worse about how he had talked to her and he thought, *Well...I guess I learned a lesson, but probably too late. I'm sure she hates me by now.* Now he was ashamed of himself, and he felt bad for Ellie.

"I'm sorry I haven't even introduced myself. I'm Joan Simpson."

"It's a pleasure to meet you Mrs. Simpson my name is Johnathan Slade, but you can call me John." Ellie had suffered losses and he knew what that was like. He wanted to sneak out of the church quietly so he wouldn't have to face Ellie. At least now he knew her name.

"Are you single Johnathan?" Joan asked.

"Yes, I am."

"I'd like you to meet my daughter Ellie, she's single too."

Oh no, he thought and quickly said, "I should be going."

"It won't take but a second, she's really a wonderful girl." Joan motioned for Ellie to come over to where her and Johnathan were.

Ellie saw her mother waving her arm and thought, *Oh my God Mom, what are you doing?* As much as she did not want to face Johnathan, she knew it was too late. If she didn't walk over to them, she would appear rude, and her mother would want to know what was wrong with her and possibly cause a scene. Her face was flushed, and it was all she could do not to run out of the church in embarrassment. She took a deep breath and summoned her courage, and then walked over to them.

"Ellie, I'd like you to meet Mr. Slade," Joan's mother said smiling up at Johnathan.

Johnathan stuck out his hand and Ellie took it. "A real pleasure to meet you Ellie."

"A pleasure to meet you too Mr. Slade," Ellie said sheepishly in a low voice. She hoped her embarrassment wasn't showing and she crossed her arms and looked down at the floor.

"Please, call me John, or Johnathan which ever rolls off your tongue easiest," he said with a warm smile. Then he added, "I can't decide which of you is the most beautiful."

Joan blushed. "Now aren't you the charmer? That's sweet of you." Johnathan felt uncomfortable and by the look of Ellie's red face, she was too. He decided it was time to leave.

"It's been a real pleasure meeting you both. Please excuse me, I have to go. I have a dog at home that I'm sharing with someone, and I may have to get him to the park by noon where we do the exchange every Sunday. Although he seems to have a mind of his own and just pops up out of nowhere."

"You share a dog with someone? How does that work?" Joan asked perplexed.

"To tell you the truth, I have enjoyed it and the other person loves the dog as much as I do, so it works out perfect. What do you think Ellie?" He looked at Ellie.

Ellie looked over at him and forced a smile. "Yes, it sounds wonderful." She looked away towards the door wishing she were anywhere but here.

Johnathan looked over at Ellie thinking, *She really hates me. She won't even look at me.*

"Well, nice meeting both of you and I hope to see you around." He turned and left the church thinking, *What idiot would cheat on her? She probably wasn't so bad once you got to know her.* She'd had a hard life and Johnathan understood why she was leery of men.

As he was reaching the bottom of the stone steps he heard a female voice calling his name, "Mr. Slade…Johnathan."

He knew it was Ellie and he didn't feel like arguing. If she started, he was going to walk away, and he turned around facing her and smiled. "Yes?"

Ellie was at the top of the stairs and had her arms crossed looking at the ground, and then she looked up at him. "I just wanted to apologize for my behavior. I know I've been difficult with you and I'm sorry. You can have Jasper for yourself. You don't have to share him with me anymore, and I hope you can forgive me." She turned and began to climb back up the steps.

"Wait a minute Ellie."

She stopped with her back to him. "Yes?" She was biting her lip thinking he was going to tell her off and she knew she deserved it. She waited tensely as her eyes slowly became wet.

"I owe you an apology too. I'm sorry for everything I've said, and well…the names I called you. I didn't really mean it."

She turned and faced him. He could see that she was crying, and he felt like a jerk. He thought to himself, *Big man making a lady cry, and he felt ashamed.*

"I can't handle Jasper alone and I don't think Jasper will be happy not being able to see you. You know he has a mind of his own and I know he loves you. I need your help…that is, if you don't hate me enough to help me."

She laughed, "I thought you hated me." She drew out a tissue from her purse and dabbed at her eyes.

"No, I don't hate you. You know what I'd like very much?"

"What?"

"For us to be friends. Can't we just be friends?"

She relaxed and smiled, "I'd like that very much. Do you still want to share Jasper then?"

"I'm afraid we don't have much choice because it seems that Mr. Jasper is running the show." They both laughed. "I'd like to share him, but only on one condition."

"What condition?" Ellie asked, her shoulders tensed in fear of what he might say.

"That I can call you."

She relaxed and smiled. "Sure Johnathan, I'd like that. I'll give you my number." She started to get a pen from her purse.

Johnathan smiled and reminded her, "you forget, I have it on caller ID."

She was wearing a mint-green dress and a white, pearl choker-necklace around her neck. Her blonde hair cascaded down past her slim, delicate shoulders and her green dress made her eyes look like emeralds. Johnathan was stunned by her beauty.

She smiled. "Call me whenever you want, and it doesn't have to pertain to Mr. Jasper."

Chapter Eighteen

JASPER GETS BUSTED

S ome weeks had passed, and Jasper was at Ellie's house laying in the sun on the back porch enjoying the warm concrete and congratulating himself on the great job he had done. The two humans were finally talking to each other on the phone and as a matter-of-fact, he had observed them conversing on the phone almost daily. They had also met at the park several times to take Jasper for a walk, and they had even been out to eat once! They still didn't know about the hole in the fence, and they still didn't know that they lived near each other. Jasper thought, *The plan was working perfectly, however they hadn't sniffed each other yet or made those ridiculous smacking noises with their faces stuck together. But I'll fix that!*

Today was Sunday, and it was time to sneak over to Johnathan's house. Jasper looked up to make sure Ellie wasn't watching through the window and then he stood up and stretched, and then he trotted over to the hole in the fence. He looked around once more and not seeing Ellie at the window, he slipped through the hole into Johnathan's yard.

Johnathan was sitting in his yard relaxing in a lawn chair thinking about Ellie. *Was he ready for a relationship, and did he want a relationship? That was the question and the answer was yes, but only with Ellie.* He wondered if she felt the same as he did. They had met in the park several times and had taken Jasper for a walk. They had even met each other at a restaurant and had dinner, but just as friends. She was intelligent and exceptionally beautiful, and she had a very warm and caring personality which he had learned was the real Ellie. She was a tough woman, and he liked a strong woman, and he knew that growing up without a father probably forced her to be strong. She had a great sense of humor and he had decided that he liked her a lot. No, more than a lot. *But what did she feel about him?*

Then his thoughts turned to Jasper. *How did he know where he and Ellie lived and how did he get from one house to another so easily?* Her house couldn't be more than twenty minutes from here, that's about the shortest time he had estimated between Jasper's disappearance and when he or Ellie, would call each other to let the other know that Jasper was at his destination. A twenty-minute radius could be anywhere in town because after all, it was a small town. Apparently Jasper knew what to do, and they didn't have to worry about him because it seemed he was quite capable of going from one house to another safely. He surmised that Jasper was very cunning, and Ellie had mentioned that he had been a stray. Jasper seemed to be a free spirit, *but how did he wind up in the river?*

Johnathan's concentration was caught by a movement at the fence. He noticed the bushes shaking and then he saw Jasper's little black, round eyes and black nose slowly appear out from behind the bushes. Jasper saw Johnathan and stopped and stared as if he thought that if he just froze in place, Johnathan would not see him. "Jasper! What are you doing in the bushes? You're supposed to be with Ellie at her house. You little rascal, come over here boy."

Oh no! Jasper thought. *I've been caught.* Jasper slowly came out from behind the bushes with his head down.

"How did you get here?" Johnathan became curious and thought, *Why was Jasper in the bushes? He certainly wasn't there when he came outside, and he'd been outside for over half an hour. Surely Jasper hadn't been hiding in the bushes that long.* Jasper walked over to Johnathan with his head down and his tail between his legs. "Oh, you are so guilty, and so busted!" Johnathan said laughing. He got up and went over to the fence and pushed the bushes apart and he found the hole. "Well, you little stinker." Johnathan had to laugh. "You're pretty slick, aren't you!?"

Now that Johnathan was up close to the fence, he could see through the small cracks in between the slats of the stockade fence and he saw Ellie! Her house was no more than forty yards away and as he watched her, he admired how beautiful she was. She was wearing a pair of white shorts and a yellow short-sleeved shirt. Her long, slender legs were tan and muscular, and he couldn't believe how beautiful she was. He saw her looking around the yard and he knew exactly who she was looking for.

He stared at Jasper and smiled saying, "you know too much don't you? Yea, you know more than you're letting on, you're just too smart for your own fuzzy pants." He chuckled. "You been playing us all this time haven't you?" Jasper looked at him sheepishly. "Oh yea, you're a real con-man, or should I say *con-dog*?" he said smiling. *What a smart dog I have! Oh, that's right...we have*. Johnathan smiled thinking of Ellie. "We're going to have to tell your mother about this I'm afraid."

Jasper whined and sat down looking at Johnathan with his long ears sticking straight in the air and Johnathan laughed. He looked back through the fence as he pulled his phone out and called Ellie. He watched as she took the phone out of her pocket and answered.

"Hello Johnathan. Jasper has run off again so watch for him, I'm sure he's on his way to your place."

"Ellie, I want to show you something."

"Where are you?"

"Do me a favor," he said laughing.

"What's so funny Johnathan?"

God, he loved it when she spoke his name! "Do you have a tall wooden stockade fence in your backyard?"

"Well yes, I do…how did you know that?" she asked mystified by his strange question.

"Could you walk up to the fence?"

"Why would you ask such a strange request? Are you alright Johnathan?"

"I'm more than alright and I think you're going to be surprised. Please Ellie, just do as I ask."

"Ok, it's a strange request but I'll trust you," she said as she started to walk across the yard towards the fence. When she got to the fence she spoke into the phone, "I'm at the fence Johnathan, now what?"

"I'm going to hang up now," Johnathan said.

"What?" She heard the phone go dead. *What's he up to, did he get cut off?* Then she heard Johnathan call her name.

"Ellie!"

At first, she put the phone back to her ear and then she heard Johnathan laughing behind the fence. She looked through the fence and saw Johnathan.

"Johnathan! What in the world are you doing behind the fence?"

"I live here," he answered laughing.

"What? You live behind the fence?"

"No, I've been renting the house back here all this time!"

"What, really? All this time?" she said laughing.

"Yes, can you believe it? Now look down in the bushes, I've solved the missing Jasper case." He was still laughing. Ellie pushed the bushes apart and saw a small hole in the fence big enough for Jasper to go through. Johnathan stuck his hand through the hole. "That's how he's been traveling from your house to mine undetected and getting back and forth so quickly. We've been had."

"That little shyster!" she said laughing. "I can't believe it. He's outsmarted us both."

"Yea, he's real slick and he's sitting over here with his head down. He knows he's been caught." Johnathan and Ellie burst out laughing.

Johnathan hesitated. "I have an idea."

Ellie smiled and bit her lip. "I don't know what it is, but I like it already."

"Would you like to come over? I'll cook a nice dinner, for all three of us."

"Only if you let me help."

Jasper perked up and wagged his tail thinking, *I did it! I just hope they understand that I'm the leader of this pack.*

Johnathan looked down at Jasper and asked, "who's taking care of who?"

Chapter Nineteen

A BRAND-NEW DAY

Within a month, the whole town knew that Ellie and Johnathan had become close friends, and they were relieved. Ellie was no longer the little spit-fire and as a matter of fact, she was rather pleasant once again like she used to be before her divorce.

It was Sunday morning and Johnathan's phone rang. He knew it was Ellie and although he had made some friends in town, he knew Ellie's number and he answered. "Hello."

"Hey!"

"Hey!" he answered back.

"I was just wondering if you wanted to go to church with the Demon lady this morning?"

"Well…let's see…"

"I'm going to hang up," Ellie teased.

He threw his head back and laughed. "I guess so, if you don't mind being seen with a Hillbilly."

"Why I'd be honored Suh," she said feigning the voice of a Southern genteel lady. "You can ride with me."

"I'll be over in a few," he said laughing.

They began to attend church together and everyone in town noticed that they were together quite often as of late. And of course, Jasper was usually with them.

They bought Jasper a green collar with his name on it and some sweaters for winter-time. He had gone from a stray dog to living like a king.

Yes, Jasper thought, *the plan was working out very well.* And he had to admit to himself that he was a regular genius.

Chapter Twenty

THE CHANCE

E llie and Johnathan continued walking Jasper together in the park and had been out to eat on several more occasions, but only as friends. They both began to have strong feelings toward each other but were afraid to tell each other. Ellie was afraid of falling in love with Johnathan and then getting dumped, and Johnathan had fears of losing Ellie like he lost his family and Petey. Neither one had told the other one how they truly felt and had kept the relationship on a friendly basis, using Jasper as an excuse to call each other and meet in the park.

Johnathan decided he wanted to take their relationship a bit further and he called Ellie to ask her out on a real date. He was a bit nervous and somewhat timid, but he knew he had fallen in love with her and he thought that maybe she felt the same about him. He decided to take a chance and call her and ask her out on a real date and if she declined, then he would know how she really felt about him. He summoned his nerve and pushed the button on the speed dial and took a deep breath and exhaled. It was Johnathan's week to keep Jasper and he was sitting on the couch resting his head on the arm of the couch looking at Johnathan. Jasper lifted his head and turned his head towards the window towards Ellie's house and then looked back at Johnathan and whined. Johnathan looked at Jasper and said, "what? I'm calling her already!" Jasper put his head back down on the arm of the couch and continued to stare at Johnathan.

Ellie answered the phone. "Hello Johnathan."

"Hey Ellie, I wanted to ask you something." He swallowed hard.

"Well, ask me something," she said laughing.

"Would you like to go out…ah…on a date…I mean like a real date…ah not just like friends?" He was tongue-tied and he thought, *What a stupid thing to say.*

The phone was silent for a moment.

"You mean like a date where people date because they have feelings for each other?" Ellie put her hand to her forehead thinking, *That was a dumb thing to say!*

"Well…yes, I guess…I mean… yes, a real date." Johnathan felt clumsy and knew he was fumbling his words.

"Can I think about that for a day or so before I answer?" Then she shook her head in disgust and thought, *Why did I say that?*

"Of course," Johnathan said thinking, *I thought so, she doesn't think of me in the same way.* "Ok, I'll see you in the park on Sunday then," he said making a face and he quickly hung up. That didn't go well at all, but at least now he knew that she didn't feel the same way he did, and he felt disappointed.

Ellie was mad at herself because she had fallen in love with him but was scared to tell him. He probably thinks that she *really* was crazy now. She should have said yes but the question took her by surprise, even though she knew it was coming sooner or later, but she was still hesitant about another relationship with any man. She was confused and decided to call her mother.

Joan was home watching television when the phone rang, and she answered the phone. "Hello."

"Hello Mom."

"Hey honey, how are you?"

"I have a question I need to ask you."

"What is it Ellie? Are you ok? Is Jasper and Johnathan alright?" Joan had kept Jasper several times when Ellie and Johnathan had gone out to eat and she had fallen in love with him.

"We're all fine Mom."

"What is it?"

"Johnathan has asked me out on a real date."

"I thought you two had already gone out on a date?" she asked perplexed.

"Those were friend dates, not a couple's date."

"What in the world are you talking about? A date is a date, you young kids have some strange ideas about romance. Did you accept?"

"I told him I would get back to him, so I didn't say yes or no. What should I do Mom?"

"What should you do? Why that's easy. You either say yes or no. But yes, would have been the right answer."

"I'm scared to say yes. What if it gets serious and then he leaves me?"

"Are you asking me if you should go out on a *real* date as you call it, or are you asking me that if you two get serious, do I think that he'll leave you?"

"I guess I'm asking you if you think he'll leave me."

"The only way you'll ever know the answer to that question is to go out with him, otherwise you'll never know the answer. If you say no, you will never know the answer to your question, only because you didn't try."

"What if he hurts me like the others did?"

"Well, you can either sit around being lonely the rest of your life and always wondering whether or not it would have worked, or you can go find out the answer to your question for yourself, then you'll know… and Ellie?"

"Yes?"

"I don't think you're going to find a man better than Johnathan."

"Thanks Mom." Ellie hung up. She was still hesitant, but she knew her mother was right.

Joan looked at the phone after Ellie hung up thinking, *Real date? What's wrong with these silly young kids today?* She shook her head and said a prayer for both of them and then added one for Jasper thinking, *That poor dog had to put up with those two.*

Ellie called Johnathan back. *What if he changed his mind?*

Johnathan answered his phone with some trepidation. "Hello."

"Hello Johnathan. Is that date offer still open?"

"Yes, it is." He crossed his fingers.

"Well then, I'd love to go out with you on a real date." She hesitated, "Johnathan?"

"Yes?"

"I'm glad we're friends."

"Ellie, we've always been friends you just didn't know it."

93

Chapter Twenty-One

TIME TO GO

J ohnathan and Ellie went on their date and the following morning when Johnathan woke up, he was not feeling well. He thought maybe it was a cold, or maybe the flu, or something he had eaten. He didn't tell anyone, but towards the end of the week he was feeling worse and he thought that maybe he should go see Doctor Bill. Ellie had mentioned to him that he didn't look well and had asked him several times if he felt ok and Johnathan told her he was fine, and then he changed the subject. She looked at him and she could tell that he was beginning to lose some of the weight he had gained back and finally she said, "Johnathan, I'm worried about you. Would you please go see Doctor Bill?"

"Alright, I call him."

He made an appointment with the Doctor and the following day he was sitting in the examination room. Doctor

Bill was a little concerned but didn't want to say anything until he ran some tests.

"What is it Doc?" Johnathan asked.

"I am going to schedule you for some tests today and when we're through, just go home and relax and take it easy until I get the results of your tests. I can't make any diagnosis until I've seen the test results."

"Ok Doc, whatever you say."

After the tests were completed Johnathan left and when Doctor Bill returned to his office he sat at his desk and looked up towards the ceiling and said, "Lord I don't know what you're doing, but I guess I'll just have to trust you."

Chapter Twenty-Two

THAT'S THE WAY IT IS

The following day Johnathan was back in the examination room waiting for the doctor to come in. Doctor Bennett tapped on the door and as he entered the room he greeted John. "Hello John."

"Hello Doctor, is everything alright? You sounded strange on the phone when you called."

"How do you feel John."

"I seem to have a stomachache sometimes and indigestion some nights, and a little weak like I don't have the energy I used to have, why? Do I have an ulcer or something?"

The Doctor looked down and then back up at Johnathan. "Your tests have come back, and I don't know how to tell you this John."

"It's easy, just tell me," he said laughing nervously.

Doctor Bill took a deep breath. "There's no easy way to tell you this John, so I'm just going to say it," he hesitated, "you have cancer and it's very advanced."

John laughed and said, "well, I'll just take chemo-therapy, right?"

"It's not that simple John. Like I said it's very far advanced."

"How did I get it?"

"Maybe from the chemicals they used in Iraq, who knows? Maybe genetic. Anyone in your family have cancer?"

"Not that I know of." John summoned up his courage and asked, "so, I just give up and die?"

"We could try chemotherapy but I'm afraid it's gone past that point and that would only make you sicker than what you are. I'm so sorry John, the best we can do is admit you into the hospital and keep you comfortable and help control the pain until..."

"How long have I got?"

"It's hard to say."

"Well say anyway."

He pressed his lips together. "Two, maybe three months at most."

"How long will I able to function normally?"

"Maybe another week or so, and that's a big maybe. The pain will get worse, but sooner or later you'll have to check into the hospital and stay."

"I've escaped death several times, but I guess it's caught up with me this time. I don't want anyone to know about this. Let this be our secret Doc."

"Aren't you going to tell Ellie? You two have been hitting it off pretty well lately."

"No! Especially not her, she's had enough pain in her life."

"John, she's going to find out sooner or later."

"I'd rather it be later. There's no use to worry her until I absolutely have to."

"I'm not sure if you realize it or not, but she's very much in love with you. All she talks about is how wonderful you are, and I don't believe I've ever seen her this happy."

John squinted his eyes and stared out the window as if he were looking at something far away. "Yes, I know, and I love her." He smiled half-heartedly adding, "and Jasper too." He had to be brave and try not to let his emotions show.

"That's the way it is Doc, there aren't any guarantees in this life. Is it true Doc what the Bible says?"

These were the times that Bill hated being a doctor. "What's that John?"

"Not sure the exact words but goes something like this, to be absent of the body is to be in the arms of Jesus." Johnathan swallowed hard fighting the tears.

"Yes John, that's exactly what it says, and you can believe it with all your heart."

"Doc, let's just keep this our secret, please."

"You want to check in now? You look pretty weak."

"No, I got a couple of things to do first."

"Sure John, whenever you're ready there will be a bed waiting for you."

"Even then, I want it to be kept a secret."

"Sure John, whatever you say."

Chapter Twenty-Three

LEAVING BREEZEWOOD

When Johnathan arrived home, he put his keys and wallet on the kitchen counter and went into the living room and sank down in the green lazy boy. He put his hands on the cushioned arms and reclined back and thought, *Well, this is it God I'm ready to go home*.

Several days later, Johnathan had become very weak and he knew he couldn't fool anyone anymore, especially Ellie. He had avoided Ellie telling her he had the flu. It was Saturday and he knew it was time to do his disappearing act and check into the VA Hospital. It hurt knowing he had to lie to Ellie and all the people he'd gotten to know here in Breezewood. Ellie would be upset and mad at him, but this was the best way. He would simply leave her a note telling her that he had decided to leave town, telling her that he wasn't ready for a relationship right now. He wished she still hated him and thought, *Maybe I could do something to make her hate me. No, that was no good.* He decided to call Bill and tell him he was ready to come in and die. He picked up the phone and dialed the number.

Bill answered the phone. "Hello John, how are you doing?"

"Not good Doc. When I woke up this morning I was really weak and sick. It's like it just hit me suddenly."

"Are you coming in?"

"Yes but…" John hesitated.

"No one needs to know where you are."

"I'm leaving Ellie a letter to tell her that I'm just not ready for a relationship and I'm moving back to Virginia where I grew up, and I need you to go along with it."

"John I can't lie, not to Ellie. I knew her before she was born, I delivered her. She's like a daughter to me."

"There's only two ways for this to end. You tell her I got the cancer and I'm dying, or my story. I'm not asking you to lie to her Bill, I'm asking you to protect her. It will be less painful my way. We have to pick the lesser of the two evils. I'm writing her a letter, that's the best way to do it and then I'll be in. I'll be at your house within the hour."

Bill sighed. "Ok John."

"See you in a bit." John hung up.

Bill put his hands together and looked up at the ceiling. "I did what you asked, and I put John in the house behind hers, so why are you taking him now? I just don't understand." He put his head down. "Forgive me Lord, your will be done, not mine."

Chapter Twenty-Four

THE LETTER WITH NO STAMP

J ohnathan thought a letter would be better than face to face. It would be so much cleaner with no tears or goodbyes. He got some paper and a pen and sat down at the table and began to write.

Dear Ellie,

I am writing this letter instead of telling you in person because it will be much easier. Face to face would have been too emotional for both of us. Take care of yourself and Jasper. I have thought about us and our friendship, and I want you to know that I have strong feelings for you, and the thought of a commitment scares me. I know this is an old cliché, but it isn't you, it's me. No use to look for me, as I have gone back to Virginia to live. Please don't be upset with me. You'll always be my closest friend. Please give Jasper a hug and a kiss for me. I will never forget you, or Jasper.

Your Friend Always,
Johnathan

"I never was good with writing letters, but I guess this will do," he said to himself as he folded the letter and slid it into an envelope. He tucked the flap into the envelope and then he wrote on the front of the envelope: "To My Best Friend Ellie".

It was Saturday and he knew Ellie would be leaving anytime now to visit her mother as she always did, and he knew Jasper was at her house, so he didn't have to worry about him. Walking was becoming a chore and he was very weak. He went out back and slowly walked up to the fence and peered through the crack. After a couple of minutes, he saw Ellie come out and get in her car and drive away. Johnathan walked around front and walked the short distance to Ellie's house. He walked over to her mailbox and placed the letter inside as tears began to fill his eyes. "Goodbye Ellie, I love you," he mumbled to himself.

He got in the car and drove to Bill's house, driving the car into the garage and shutting the garage door so that Ellie or no one else could see it. He went up to Bill's house and knocked on the door. Doctor Bill opened the door and looked at Johnathan. "Ready John?"

"Yes, let's go."

Johnathan and Bill climbed into Bill's SUV and headed to the VA Hospital. Once there, Bill checked Johnathan in and took him to his room.

"Make yourself comfortable John and if there's anything at all that I can do just tell the nurse. And if you need me, she will call me immediately. Of course, I will be in often to check on you."

"Thanks Bill."

The Doctor left and Johnathan shut the door and then he sat in the chair by the bed for almost an hour letting his mind wander and eventually he looked up at the clock thinking, *Ellie was probably reading his letter by now*, and tears began to fall from his gaunt face.

Chapter Twenty-Five

THE FINAL DREAM

When Ellie returned home from her mother's house she parked her car in the gravel driveway and went to the mailbox. She saw an envelope with no stamp that was addressed only as, "To My Best Friend Ellie" and she had a bad feeling about the envelope as she opened it and began to read the words that tore her heart out. She ran into her house and fell on her bed face down crying. *Why? What was wrong with her? Why couldn't she keep a man?* This time was different though, she wasn't mad, and she had no hate in her heart. There was only a deep sense of loss and sadness and she felt lethargic, as if a piece of her soul were missing. She thought that when she had met her husband that she knew love, but now she realized that she had never known real love, until she met Johnathan. She knew he was the only one for her and she had thought that he had felt the same about her. No, she thought to herself, she had never known real love until Johnathan came into her life. *What was she going to do now?* She fell asleep sobbing.

Ellie began to dream, and she found herself back in the vacant house. Everything was the same and she waited for the dream to progress. There was Belle and the Wolf-dog in the usual place, and by now she had realized that the Wolf-dog was Johnathan's dog Petey. She looked to the left and Johnathan was sitting on the couch like before and he looked frail and weak.

"Johnathan, why have you left me? I love you," she said through tears.

"Why Ellie...I'm dying."

"Dying, how? What's wrong?"

"Like your father," he said in a distant sounding voice as he began to fade away until he was gone.

"Johnathan, come back!" she begged, "I love you, don't you leave me now. I need you. You're the only one I'll ever love!" Ellie woke up screaming, "come back, I won't let you die!"

She sat up shaking and looked at the phone. She picked up the phone and called Doctor Bill's number.

Doctor Bill was reluctant to answer the phone. He knew it was Ellie and he had dreaded this moment, and he knew he couldn't lie very well. He answered and tried to sound nonchalant and happy. "Hello Ellie," he said, and then swallowed hard. His mouth was suddenly as dry as cotton.

"Doctor Bill where's Johnathan?"

He could tell she was upset, and he knew she was crying. Apparently, she had read John's letter. "Oh, ah gee…I guess he's at home. Have you tried calling him?"

"Don't play games with me Bill!" she said angrily.

"Why Ellie whatever are you talking about?" He covered his face with his free hand.

"Johnathan is dying, isn't he?" she said matter-of-factly.

This shocked and surprised Bill and he blurted out, "how did you know?" Then he stuttered saying, "I…I mean, what in the world makes you think that Ellie." Oh no, he thought. *How did she know?*

"Where is he Bill? Tell me right now, or I swear I'm coming over there and it won't be pleasant."

He could tell she was mad and everyone in town knew that you didn't mess with Ellie when she got mad, and by now everyone knew that Johnathan had left.

"Look, ok I'm sorry but that's how John wanted it."

"Why?" she said in a hurt voice.

"Because he wanted you to think he left, rather than telling you he was dying. He…we chose the lesser of the two evils. He didn't want to hurt you any more than he had to. He did it out of concern for your well-being and we both decided this was the best way."

"Is he in the VA Hospital Bill?"

"Yes Ellie, we thought that…" Ellie hung up before Bill could finish his sentence and he decided he'd better get to the hospital before she tore the place apart.

Ellie looked in the mirror, fluffed her hair and decided she looked good enough. She got in her car and sped to the hospital. She knew for certain now that she loved Johnathan more than anything else, and she wasn't going to let him die alone.

Chapter Twenty-Six

NO TIME FOR SPEED LIMITS

E llie pushed the gas pedal down as far as it would go. She was breaking the speed limit but didn't care. Dave the town police officer had set up his radar just outside of town, hiding behind a billboard. He saw the white sports car zoom past and his radar indicated ninety miles per hour as Ellie flashed by, and the speed limit was fifty-five. He knew it was Ellie, because everyone knew who drove the only white sports car in town. He just sat there thinking to himself, *I'm not going to stop her, she's angry. No sir, he wasn't going to pull her over, he'd rather mess with a rattlesnake than to mess with Ellie*. He pretended he didn't see her and quickly reset the radar.

Louis the mailman had stopped to deliver Ellie's mail and had seen the un-stamped envelope. He noticed it was not sealed and the flap was tucked in, so he decided to read it and when he finished reading it, he replaced it and then he took off to warn everyone to beware of Ellie; she had been left by a man again.

Ellie arrived at the hospital and rushed up to the main desk and demanded to know where Johnathan Slade's room was.

"I'm sorry miss, that's confidential infor…"

Ellie interrupted her with a look on her face that could kill. "I said, what room is Johnathan Slade in?"

The secretary had seen her coming, and had moved her hand under the desk ready to push the panic button to call security just as Doctor Bill walked in. "It's ok Tammy, I'll take care of this."

Ellie turned to Bill. "Take me to him Bill. Now!"

"Ok Ellie, calm down."

"I won't calm down!"

"If you just calm down, I'll take you to him."

Her face relaxed a little and she followed the Doctor to the elevator. "He's on the fourth floor, private room number 12."

They got off the elevator and walked down the wing to room twelve. Johnathan was lying in bed reading the Bible that he had found in the bedside drawer and he looked up when Doctor Bill walked in. "John, there's someone here to see you."

"What! Who? I thought we agreed to…"

Ellie pushed her way around Bill and the anger faded from her face and was quickly replaced with worry and sadness, and she was on the verge of crying.

"Johnathan! Oh my God, why didn't you tell me?"

Johnathan was surprised and tried to sit up in the bed but was too weak. Ellie was the last person he had expected to come through that door. "Ellie, what are you doing here? I didn't want you to see me like this, I didn't want you to know."

"It's too late now. I'm staying...unless you want me to leave."

"No, I don't want you to leave and now that you're here, I'm glad."

She sat down in the chair beside him and leaned toward him. She took his hand and said, "I'm staying here as long as you want me to." Tears began to well up in her eyes. Johnathan saw Ellie's tears and his eyes began to glisten with the tears he was desperately trying to hold back.

"Please don't cry Ellie," Johnathan pleaded. "It hurts me to see you cry. I'm sorry for leaving, but I thought it best for you."

"I'll decide what's best for me."

He knew better than to argue with her. He looked at her and he knew without a doubt that he loved her and although they had never told each other, he knew that she loved him too, but it was a little too late now.

Chapter Twenty-Seven

THE RETURN OF FAITH

Ellie sat with Johnathan until late in the evening and when she looked up at the clock, it was eleven p.m. She looked at Johnathan and he looked tired and weak. "I'm going to leave and let you get some rest, but I'll be back early tomorrow right after church. I have to feed Jasper. I'm sure he probably thinks I've deserted him."

"Hug him for me, will you?"

"You know I will."

John hesitated, "I'm sorry Ellie."

"You don't have to say you're sorry Johnathan."

"Thanks."

She smiled affectionally at him. "You don't have to thank me either."

The Doctor came in to see how Johnathan was doing before he left. "Do you two need anything before I leave?" They were both just staring at each other and were oblivious to the Doctor. "Ok," he muttered to himself and he left them alone, shutting the door behind him as he left.

After several seconds Ellie turned to the book Johnathan had been reading. "You're reading the Bible?"

"Yes. I'll never give up my faith, no matter how bad things get."

Ellie said good-by and left the room and as she got on the elevator, the bell chimed, and the door closed. She pushed the first-floor button and thought, *Maybe it's time I got my faith back.*

Chapter Twenty-Eight

ELLIE NEEDS A MIRACLE

When Ellie returned home, Jasper jumped on her pawing her legs and wagging his tail. She set her keys and purse down immediately and picked Jasper up and hugged him. She kissed him and kissed him a second time saying, "and this one's from your Daddy."

Jasper seemed to know that something was wrong with Johnathan and he wondered why he hadn't seen him in a several days, and he wondered where he was. Jasper knew Johnathan was not at his house and he looked at Ellie and whined thinking, *Where is Johnathan?* Ellie looked at Jasper and said, "you know something's not right don't you baby?" His long ears perked up and he looked at Ellie. "Don't worry, it's going to be alright," she said, and she began to cry and then she got on her knees and began to pray. And Jasper sat beside her.

The next morning Ellie went to church a few minutes early and she caught Bill before the service started. "Bill could I have a moment with you?"

"Sure Ellie, what can I do for you?"

"Would you ask all the people in the congregation to pray for Johnathan to be healed."

Bill stood there in shock. "Why Ellie, praise God you've found your faith again."

Ellie's face turned red. "Yes, if Johnathan believes as much as he does in his condition, then who am I to doubt."

"Well I'll be...yes we will do that absolutely! I had planned to ask for prayers, but our prayers will be stronger with you joining in."

Before the ending of the service, Pastor Bill told everyone of Johnathan's diagnosis and the whole congregation prayed for his recovery. He told everyone that there would be a prayer vigil for Johnathan every evening here in the church at six o'clock, and then he added looking at Ellie, "It's prayer warrior time in Breezewood!"

Several weeks had passed, and Ellie visited Johnathan every day. She stayed with him each day until visiting hours were over. One morning she noticed that Johnathan was looking somewhat better. The color had begun to come back in his face, and he seemed to be more alert.

"How are you feeling Johnathan?"

He furrowed his brow. "You know, I have been feeling somewhat better lately. Must be the hospital food," he said laughing.

She forced a smile. "I very much doubt that. You know Johnathan, that's the first I've heard you laugh in a long time." She stared at Johnathan and couldn't believe how much she loved him and how handsome he was, even in his decimated state.

"You're right, it is. I haven't laughed in...well, I don't know how long." He stared at Ellie and became sad and looked away. It was a shame he was dying. He really believed that they could have had a wonderful life together.

Ellie saw the sadness in his face. "What's wrong Johnathan?"

"Nothing."

The door opened and a nurse brought Johnathan's lunch in and set it on the table. "Lunch time!" she said and smiled at them both.

After Johnathan had eaten all the food, he laughed and told Ellie they hadn't been bringing enough food lately, and he said jokingly, "I'm not dead yet."

That's odd she thought, *He hasn't eaten much lately and now he's starving. I need to talk to Bill, maybe something is wrong. What would the last stages be like? Would a person have more of an appetite and start to laugh in his last days? Do the last stages of cancer cause a psychological change towards the end to cause this behavior? Was it his faith that allowed him to accept death?* She tried to remember the last days of her father's bout with cancer, but she couldn't remember because she had been too young, and it had been so many years ago. She was worried that Johnathan was close to death and she shuttered to think of him dying. She knew he was dying, but she refused to accept it. She would talk with Doctor Bill.

"When was the last time Bill was here to see you?"

"I don't know. Maybe yesterday, why?"

"Oh nothing, just wondered. Could you excuse me, I have to go to the bathroom. I'll be right back."

She left the room and went out into the hall and pulled her phone out of her pocket and called Bill.

"Hello Ellie, is something wrong? I've been busy and I've been meaning to get up to see John. And as a matter of fact, I'm on my way up now. What's up?"

"I'm not really sure. His behavior is strange, could I talk to you?"

"What do you mean, strange?"

"I'm not sure. Could I talk with you for a minute?"

"I'm on the elevator on my way up. I'll see you in a moment."

Bill exited the elevator and saw Ellie down the hall and walked up to her. "What's going on?" he asked.

"I've noticed that in the last couple of days Johnathan has been eating more, his color looks better, and he actually laughed today which he hasn't done for quite a while. Is this what happens when someone is nearing death?"

"No, that's not normal. Usually the patient gets depressed and scared, maybe it's John's faith."

"I don't think so. I'm worried Bill. Could you run those tests again as soon as possible...for me, please?"

Bill looked at Ellie and felt sorry for her. "Sure Ellie, I'll schedule some tests today."

"I want every test available, please Bill."

He knew that tests were useless at this point, but he looked into her eyes and he knew better than to argue, it was just easier to do what she asked. "Ok Ellie, I'll run the whole gamut on him again."

"Thanks Bill."

Chapter Twenty-Nine

THE TOWN COMES TOGETHER

B ill was in his office when the results came back. He looked at the blood test results and shook his head. He turned on the X-ray screen lights and slid each X-ray upwards onto the screen until the clips held the pictures in place. He examined the X-rays and was baffled. He stared at the black and white X-rays for several seconds and then he went over to the phone and called Arlene in the X-ray department.

"X-Ray department. Arlene speaking how can I help you?"

"Arlene, this is Doctor Bennett. When was the last time the X-Ray machine was calibrated?"

"Hmm…let me see. According to the service chart it was serviced and calibrated last week, why?"

"Are you sure?" he questioned.

"Yes Doctor, would like to see the service records?"

"No, that's fine."

Bill called the Ward Nurse. "I want to repeat every test that we did on Johnathan Blake this morning please, including X-rays."

"Is something wrong Doctor?"

"No, I just want it done again."

"You want the tests done today?"

"Yes, please. I don't believe the last tests were correct."

"Yes sir, right away Doctor."

"Thanks."

He hung up the phone and turned around in his chair facing the X-rays staring at them for several seconds, and then he looked up at the ceiling. "Please God, don't tease me." He took his round rimmed glasses off and wiped the pesky tears from his eyes.

He went back upstairs to Johnathan's room. "Johnathan, I've ordered another round of tests again for you today."

"What, again? Why Doc? What's the use? I'm dying, why waste time making me take those uncomfortable tests? I've already taken all your tests."

"I just want to run a few more tests again John, the last ones were inconclusive."

"No, I don't think there's any use Bill. Save it for someone who needs it."

Ellie broke in. "Please Johnathan, for me?" She looked back at Bill and knew something was up. She had known Bill all her life and he had been like a father to her after her father died, then she looked back at Johnathan.

Johnathan looked at Ellie and sighed. "Alright, for you, I'll do it."

She looked back at Bill and smiled. The nurse knocked on the door and Bill told them to come in. The nurse was followed by an orderly with a wheelchair.

Ellie said, "I'll be here when you come back Johnathan."

Johnathan smiled and said, "I'm counting on it." After he sat down in the wheelchair he asked Bill and the others if they would step out of the room for a moment so he could talk with Ellie in private. They left the room closing the door behind them. Johnathan put his hand on Ellie's slim, delicate hand. "Ellie." He stopped and swallowed.

"Yes Johnathan?" She stared at him.

"I want to tell you something and please don't interrupt me until I'm through, or I'll never finish."

"What is it Johnathan?"

"I'm sorry I left like I did, but I didn't want to hurt you anymore than I had to and well…"

"I'm listening Johnathan." She took his hand in hers.

"Ah…I'll just come out and say it. I think I've fallen in love with you."

"I know," she said smiling.

"You do?"

"Yes, and I've been wanting to tell you that I love you too."

"It's a little late for us now isn't it?" he said forcing a smile.

"No, it isn't. You know what they say, better late than never and it's what I've been wanting to hear for a while now."

"You have?"

"Yes, knowing you love me will make it easier when… you know."

"When I die?"

"Please don't say that word Johnathan."

The Doctor knocked on the door and said, "let's go you two."

"How long will this take Doc," Johnathan asked.

"We should be done by four o'clock."

"I'll be here waiting for you Johnathan," Ellie said.

They took Johnathan down the hall in the wheelchair as Bill and Ellie watched him go. "This will take a while Ellie you should go get something to eat."

"What is it Bill?"

"His last tests were inconclusive, and I decided to run them again."

"What do you mean?"

"It means something may be wrong with the last tests."

"*All* the tests were wrong? How could that be? Are you just telling me this to appease me?"

"No Ellie. I want to run them again. Just keep praying."

"Are you sure there's something you're not telling me?"

"No Ellie. I won't know anything until these new tests come back, now go get something to eat."

Chapter Thirty

A LESSON LEARNED

When the second round of tests were completed Bill examined them and shook his head. He was baffled, flabbergasted, and happy all at the same time. He couldn't believe what he was seeing. All the tests came back negative. There was no cancer anywhere. Johnathan was clean and healthy, and Bill looked up at the ceiling and put his hands together. "Praise God! Thank you Lord!"

He pulled out his phone and called Ellie and she answered immediately. "What is it Bill?"

"Where are you Ellie?"

"I'm just finishing lunch in the cafeteria, why?"

"Wait there, I'll be right there." He hung up the phone and headed to the cafeteria. He saw Ellie sitting alone at a table sipping on a cup of coffee when he entered the cafeteria and he walked over and sat down.

"What's wrong Bill?"

"It's unbelievable Ellie! I just can't get over it, and I'm a Pastor."

Ellie was getting impatient. "What is it Bill? Tell me before I burst."

He looked intensely at Ellie. "It's a miracle Ellie. An honest-to-God miracle! All the tests came back clean and to make sure, you know I ran them again."

"I'm sorry Bill, when you say clean, what exactly does that mean?"

"The cancer is gone! There is no cancer, and all of John's bloodwork and all the tests are consistent with a healthy young man."

Ellie stared in disbelief for several seconds and then she began to cry. Bill's eyes became wet too when he saw Ellie's tears.

She dried her eyes with a tissue and then looked at Bill in disbelief. "Are you sure? Are you positive?"

"Yes, there's no mistake. That's why I ran the tests a second time."

"Praise God!" Ellie jumped up from her chair and set back down. People in the cafeteria were turning in their chairs to look at her, but Ellie ignored them.

Bill rubbed his chin as a thought popped into his mind. "You know what I think?"

"What?"

"I think all this was God's way of bringing you back to him. Sometimes it takes something bad to bring us back to

God and I think if you hadn't of gotten your faith back and prayed, Johnathan would have died."

Ellie stared at him and she knew in her heart and spirit that his statement was true. It all fit together. The dreams, saving Jasper, and meeting Johnathan. It was no coincidence. God had answered her prayers.

"Let's go tell John the great news," Bill said.

"Wait, I have an idea," Ellie said excitedly.

"What is it?"

Eagerly, she leaned over and told Bill her plan.

"Well, that sounds like a wonderful idea," he said with a big grin on his face. "Won't John be surprised."

Chapter Thirty-One

THE FUNERAL-WEDDING

Later that afternoon Jonathan was sitting in the chair in his room and he wondered where everyone was. *Where were Ellie and Bill? Ellie said she would be here at four o'clock and it was almost five o'clock. Had she forgotten? She said she had a surprise for him, but what could you possibly get a dying man that would surprise him?* He laughed at his morbid joke. He was feeling exceptionally good and wondered why. If this was dying, it wasn't so bad. Maybe God was easing his pain before he took him.

Several minutes later he heard a bunch of commotion up the hall and wondered what was going on. The noise was getting closer to his room and then the door opened, and Ellie and Doctor Bill came in followed by a crowd of people. Ellie was holding Jasper and she set him down. Jasper ran over and jumped in Johnathan's lap licking him and wagging his tail. So, this was the surprise.

"What a wonderful surprise! It's so good to see you Jasper!" he said, and then he hugged Jasper and kissed him.

Ellie walked over beside Johnathan and took his hand and Jasper jumped off his lap and sat staring at Ellie and Johnathan, looking back and forth. People were crowding in the room until there was no more room and there were still more people out in the hall trying to peek in. Johnathan looked around the room. "What in the world is going on?"

Bill looked at Ellie. "Tell him Ellie."

Ellie smiled at Johnathan.

"Will someone please tell me what's going on?" Johnathan demanded. "What are all these people doing here?"

"I knew something wasn't right. You were looking and feeling better, so I asked Bill to run some tests again and all your tests have come back negative."

"Negative? I don't understand," he said bewildered.

Bill threw his arms up in the air. "The cancer is gone John. Praise God! It's a miracle."

"But how? I didn't take any chemo, how's that possible?"

Ellie had tears in her eyes. "Anything is possible with God. Everyone in town prayed for you every night." Ellie squeezed his hand and Johnathan looked at her in disbelief and noticed her wet eyes looked as though they were shining.

Johnathan was stunned. No wonder he felt so good! "Thank God, and thank all of you." His eyes became wet and Ellie hugged him. He asked again, "are you sure, there's no mistake?"

Bill shook his head. "No mistake John. God has cured you and there is no other explanation."

After he collected his wits, Johnathan began laughing. "Why is half the town in my room?"

Bill looked around the room with a big smile on his face. "Why John, they're all here for the wedding."

Johnathan was confused. "What wedding, Doc?" he asked.

"Wrong. Today I'm a Pastor not a doctor, and it's *your* wedding. We figure you been fooling around long enough with our Ellie and it's time you two quit playing games and get real."

The Pastor took off his lab coat and he was wearing his frock underneath, and then he took out his Bible and said, "Do you Ellie, take Johnathan the Hillbilly to be your lawfully wedded husband?"

Ellie looked at Johnathan with a loving smile and said, "I certainly do!"

The Pastor continued, "and do you Johnathan take Ellie, the Demon lady to be your lawfully wedded wife?"

Johnathan looked at Ellie laughing and said, "with all my heart I do!"

"I now pronounce you husband and wife. You may kiss the bride."

And he did.

Jasper smiled, or what passed for a dog smile and thought, *It's about time they made those ridiculous human smacking noises!*

ABOUT THE AUTHOR

Maire Woodward resides in West Virginia with her husband Steven Woodward. She has two sons, and four grandchildren. She enjoys gardening, reading, writing poems, and spending time with her grandchildren.

Marie has published several poems and has worked in administrative/accounting positions for over 30 years and graduated from Technical School in the Medical Field.

Marie loves people and animals and currently has a Carin Terrier named Jasper.

BOOKS FOR PET LOSS AND PROOF OF THE AFTERLIFE FOR ANIMALS:

"Biblical Proof Animals Do Go To Heaven" By Steven H. Woodward (2012).

When Steven lost his beloved dog BJ he was devastated. Steven had to know if BJ was in heaven or just a pile of dust. After much praying Steven was given a vision where he was taken to heaven to see BJ and all his dogs he had owned. Read of his vision and all the proof that he was given to him that proves animals have souls and do go to heaven. A book for pet loss.

"God's Revelations Of Animals And People" By Steven H. Woodward (2017).

Since the seven years after writing his first book, Steven was given many more revelations of proof that animals do go to Heaven. His second book contains much more proof, and some of his personal visions (including the abridged vision of BJ), and answers to questions that people have asked him about his first book regarding what he saw in Heaven. He also answers questions such as, "Will my pet be raptured?" "Will I see my beloved animal in Heaven?" Also, in this book Steven dispels several myths about the Bible and reveals several secrets of the Bible. A book for pet loss.

"BJ: A Dog's Journey Into The Afterlife" By Steven H. Woodward (2018).

This is a beautiful story of the afterlife, redemption, and forgiveness for one man and one dog. It is a story of fiction based on *true divine events* that happened to Steven and his dog BJ which he writes about in his first book. But this story is told by BJ, through his eyes. In this story BJ has a near death experience and goes to Heaven but he is sent back to life on a mission; he must come back to earth and save a man he has never met. BJ is street wise and he doesn't care much for humans, but he is determined to complete his mission. This story is about BJ's journey to find this mystery man and unconditional love. Steven has endeavored to tell this story inside the mind of his dog BJ, using BJ's unique personality and character. A great book that helps people to understand how animals think and feel, which is much like us. A book that teaches young children how precious animals really are. A book for all ages. A book for pet loss.

"How to Recover From the Heartbreak of Pet Loss" By Steven H. Woodward (2019).

A book of healing words and advice. Contains both Scientific and Biblical proof that our beloved pets do go to Heaven. This book explores the facts and proofs of the afterlife, the soul, and Heaven for animals. Find out what really causes the pain, and the secrets of how animal lovers bond their souls with the souls of animals. Plus, a Ten-Step guide to help you through the difficult times. Plus, true amazing stories of people who have seen their animals in Heaven, and true stories of animals that saved humans. A book for pet loss, no matter what type of animal you have lost.

"How to Have Visions and Supernatural Knowledge in The Bible You Didn't Know Existed" By Steven H. Woodward. (2020).

Proof animals go to Heaven proven through scriptures, and the debunking of the scriptures that people try to use to make you think they don't! Arm yourself with the facts. A guide on how to have Visions and many mysteries of the Bible explained. Learn the Gospel of "Q" that has recently been found! Find out the Divine Frequencies of Heaven and learn of the Nephilim, the Giants, Aliens, and Demons; what they really are, and where they come from. Facts to know if you are truly Saved.

REFERENCES:

*King James Bible, Holman Bible Publishers; Copyright
1998. Mass market edition 005405430

CPSIA information can be obtained
at www.ICGtesting.com
Printed in the USA
LVHW050029300920
667371LV00016B/467